MIRIAM, DANIEL

AND ME

To Myra

MIRIAM, DANIEL
AND ME

EURON GRIFFITH

Seren is the book imprint of
Poetry Wales Press Ltd,
57 Nolton Street, Bridgend, Wales, CF31 3AE

www.serenbooks.com
facebook.com/SerenBooks
Twitter: @SerenBooks

This is a work of fiction. All of the characters, organisations, and events
portrayed in this novel are either products of the author's imagination or
are used ficticiously.

ISBN: 9781781725733
Ebook: 9781781725740

A CIP record for this title is available from the British Library.

The publisher acknowledges the financial assistance
of the Welsh Books Council.

Cover photograph:Model with felt hat by Marka, Alamy.

Printed by Severn, Gloucester

Our lives are merely trees of possibilities

– Marc Bolan

ONE

God lived with us in Llys Meifor. Nain had told me. Wrapped in black shawls she was a giant spider in the corner of the room railing at whatever came on the television that was in any way fun or betraying the slightest hint of liberation.

Which of course meant everything I loved.

The Monkees and *Thunderbirds* mainly. Nain said that they were all going to Hell. She would declaim that All The Sinners Would Burn Forever In Flames The Size Of Mountains. I felt a bit sad for the Spencer Davis Group and Lady Penelope as they flickered on our telly oblivious to their Ultimate Fate. But Nain knew a lot about God. She spoke to him.

"You spoke to *God?*"

"Of course."

"When?"

"All the time. He's all around."

"He's here *now?* In the *larder?*"

Nain smiled.

"Yes."

I looked around the shelves at the fruits of Nain's industry. Jars of piccalilli, marmalade, strawberry jam, mustard, pickled cabbage. Tins of Welsh cakes, scones, biscuits, apple tarts and ginger snaps. In the far corner, huge hams were tucked away and covered in muslin.

But I couldn't see God.

"Is he *big* Nain?"

"Big as Snowdon."

"So how can he fit into the larder?"

"Because he can also be as small as a mouse. And he can change shapes too. You see this jar of milk? When I pour it into this small cup it changes shape doesn't it? It's still milk, but it's smaller. God is like that."

"God is like *milk?*"

"In a way."

"So can I drink him?"

"What did Dr Rees say? Can you remember?"

Dr Ffrancon-Rees, the white-haired minister at Bethel chapel was seven hundred years old. He was always talking about God. In his sing-song voice in chapel he'd said that only the Pure in Heart could hear God's words. I had no idea if I was Pure in Heart but I did try to be good. I always helped my Mum with her clothes pegs when she was putting up the washing. I brushed my teeth three times a day. I even ate broccoli, swallowing quickly before the taste kicked in. The way I saw it, if God really *was* everywhere then he would have spotted how good I was and made a note of it. Maybe I was Pure in Heart too. Maybe he would talk to me.

"Is God out in the garden, Nain?"

"I told you, he's everywhere. He's all around."

So I went to find him.

I quickly realised that God was good at Hide and Seek. Of course, if Nain was right then God had the advantage of being able to change his size and shape and also to become invisible when it suited him so that was no surprise. I would have called it cheating but I didn't want to upset God so I kept it to myself. I looked behind the rose bushes, avoiding the thorns, beneath the window of my Dad's study where he wrote all his poetry. Seeing me, he smiled so I decided that he must have been in a good mood. I went in.

"I'm looking for God."

Dad took off his glasses, placed them by the side of his type-writer and smiled.

"Nain said he was everywhere."

"She told me that too when I was your age."

"And did you find him?"

"No."

"He's hiding."

"Maybe."

"But why? All I want to do is talk to him for a bit."

"God is strange."

He ruffled my hair, put the glasses back on his nose and turned back to his typewriter. I knew this meant our chat was at an end.

I went out into the garden again and sat on the wall looking out into the fields. What if God was a cow? If he could change his shape why not become a cow? It was the perfect disguise. Who would suspect that one of the black and white Friesians in Mr Pierce's field was actually God? He could be there all day just munching the grass and mooing and pooing and no one would bother him. I stared at them for a bit but none of them looked very smart. Besides, I was scared of cows. Everyone said they were harmless but as soon as I got close they started ganging up and lowering their heads as if they were going to charge. I decided that if God really *was* disguising himself as a cow I would wait until he became something else. A cat maybe. Something that would jump on my lap and start purring.

But God had moved on. He was somewhere far more exciting. And I couldn't blame him.

Nothing ever happened in Bethel. No one interesting or new ever came to visit. There were never any strangers. Everyone knew each other by name. And everyone spoke Welsh.

Illya Kuryakin never spoke Welsh. Neither did Peter Tork, Davy Jones, Mickey Dolenz or Mike Nesmith. In a world where all the important and cool stuff was happening in English I began to question not only God but my entire universe. Dad had told me that Welsh was the most beautiful language in the world and that everyone in England was jealous of us and that was the reason they wanted to destroy it. But no one important spoke it. That was the trouble. If it was that beautiful why didn't the Monkees use it? The only Welsh I heard on TV was some people singing hymns on a Sunday evening. There was a bigger world out there. I'd seen it on television. So I asked my Mum.

"Where does Illya Kuryakin live?"

"America."

"Where's that?"

"Across the sea."

"Like Ireland?"

"Much further."

"Can we go?"

"It's too expensive. We would have to fly. And we'd need passports."

"Do the Monkees live in America too?"

"Yes."

"Do you think they'll ever come to Wales?"

"I don't think so."

"Why not?"

"Why should they?"

The truth struck me like a saucepan.

We didn't matter.

TWO

Miriam cried in her bedroom whilst, downstairs Alwyn – his customary drunkeness infused with Righteous Fury – yelled threats of disownment and violence. Eluned wailed, not knowing what to do or what to think – her life suddenly a shattered vase. Having had her only daughter threaten to become a Catholic and move to Ireland only a month or so earlier had been a terrifying prospect but now, seeing her pregnant out of wedlock to a man they hadn't even met was even worse. Everyone in Cysegr chapel knew about it and, on Sundays, heads were bowed in embarrassment and shame as Alwyn, Eluned and Miriam walked past in their finery, clutching their hymn books and taking their usual pew. Miriam was told by Eluned that she would have to write to Pádraig and tell him what had happened. It was her duty to tell him. As a good Catholic he might even recognise her confession and offer forgiveness although Miriam knew that forgiveness was as remote and as meaningless as Mars. Somewhere in Dublin he was waiting for her letter and looking forward to hearing about the tiny and inconsequential events of her week with Leah at the shoe shop. Her moans about the stupid customers and the monstrous Mr Oliver! It was the thing he looked forward to now that the letters had started arriving again. He had been worried for a while. He had wondered if there had been someone else. But he'd been wrong to doubt her love. The row of hastily crossed kisses at the end of her letters were all the proof he needed. And the hint of perfume too. In one letter there had even been a pressed wild violet from one of the Pantglyn fields. He'd written back telling her about the cottage they would buy one day on the cliffs. They would have a dog. And enough straw bobbies to fill a whole house just like he'd promised. A small cottage maybe. Although definitely not a mansion.

None of it mattered now. None of it would happen. There would be no more letters.

And it was her own stupid fault.

Twenty-two year old Pádraig came from Dublin and was very good with his hands. There was nothing he couldn't fix. Fridges, phones, crooked bookshelves, cars – everything was a challenge and whatever Alwyn or Eluned presented him with would be carefully assessed and inspected before being returned to them in as good a condition, if not better, than its original state. Watching young Pádraig fit a plug onto the new food mixer was like watching a vet coolly perform a life-saving procedure on some tiny animal, tucking in the wires like troublesome intestines whilst occasionally puffing the ginger fringe from his face.

"There you go Mrs Walters, that should see you right."

Alwyn would have messed it up. Fiddled for ages. Complained about the screwdriver. Scrambled around the toolbox noisily spitting out words which would never be heard within fifty yards of Cysegr chapel. There were times when Alwyn would have loved to smash his young lodger in the face. But everyone in Pantglyn adored Pádraig. When he smiled it really did feel as if the chilly Caernarfonshire wind had stopped for a few seconds and as if the place had suddenly got warmer. When the words tumbled out of his mouth it sounded like a pleasing arpeggio on a harp. He'd only been there for a couple of months, lodging in Carneddi – the Walters' terraced cottage – whilst he worked as an apprentice electrician in a small firm just outside Caernarfon, but in that time Pádraig had made the village of Pantglyn a nicer place. No one had an unkind word. The men in the pub loved him. Even the local minister loved him.

But nobody loved him more than Miriam.

In the beginning she had been quite antagonistic. Why did they need a lodger? No one else in Pantglyn had one. And she had always liked having a spare room next to her own. It was her special place. Somewhere to run to when she wanted the world to go away or when Alwyn's drinking had gone too far and he was throwing things around downstairs and shouting at Eluned. Now that sanctuary was gone and, worse, she had to be on her best behaviour in the morning at the breakfast table. All because of a stupid Irishman.

Love came as a shock. As unexpected as a wolf in a parlour. Naturally, as a young girl of eighteen, she'd read about love in her magazines and she'd seen it on the screen of the Majestic cinema in Caernarfon but real love was different. It was something she felt. Like stomach ache or dizziness. No magazine or film had told her that. It seeped into every part of her body and every part of her day. Even the act of walking to the bus stop every morning was something she now had to think about because that mechanical and previously automatic action of placing one foot in front of another whilst swinging her handbag now became an object of pure concentration. It reminded her of when Alwyn was drunk and when he tried to walk in a straight line to convince Eluned that he was sober. Miriam worried that, at any moment, if she wasn't careful, she would crash into a wall and draw attention to herself or, equally possible, she might just float up from the pavement entirely, drifting like a daft balloon up through the clouds – Pantglyn becoming insignificant matchboxes beneath her heels.

At night she would listen to the sounds from her old sanctuary. Now it was Pádraig's room and she heard the creaks from his bed. Sometimes he would hum a little song to himself, no words, just a snatch of a melody which, to Miriam, sounded as lovely as a flute. Even his snoring sounded musical. Love was turning the world into some weird and peculiar opera she couldn't quite follow.

"Have you ever been to the Fair City?"

Alwyn and Eluned had gone out for the evening. It was a warm Spring evening and Miriam and Pádraig were alone in the back garden.

"Where's the Fair City?"

Pádraig chuckled gently.

"That's what they call Dublin. It's the most beautiful city in the world. You should come with me one day. We could buy a cottage by a cliff overlooking the Irish Sea and I could make you a straw bobby every morning to keep you company while I go to work."

"What's a straw bobby?"

Pádraig ripped out a bunch of grass.

"Close your eyes."

She heard him twisting and pulling the grass until it squeaked. Then, after twenty seconds had passed, she heard his voice again.

"Okay, you can open them now."

He placed a beautifully-crafted doll, a little grass man, in her hand.

"I can make enough to fill a house," said Pádraig. He laughed. "A small cottage maybe. Although definitely not a mansion!"

Miriam laughed back as she stroked her straw bobby. But then she became serious again.

"Do you have to go?"

"It's only for a month. Maybe even less. The doctor said she was on the mend so you never know."

"I don't want you to go."

Pádraig watched her cry. He offered his hand and she took it as if it contained all the treasure in the world.

She got up carefully, took her big bag down from the top of the wardrobe and filled it with clothes, not really caring what she packed – stockings, blouses, skirts – all stuffed in, as much as she could manage. Shoes were dropped into a plastic bag. Make-up tucked into her coat pocket. Was Dublin going to be cold? Did she have enough money? She'd saved a little. She unscrewed the belly from Puw, her porcelain pig, and the coins tumbled out of his guts. Silver was judiciously separated from copper. But there was far too much copper. There was five pounds in Eluned's purse. She would borrow it. Leave a note. When she got a proper job out in Dublin she would repay the amount with interest. The suitcase wasn't too heavy. She took it down the stairs and listened to the sound of Alwyn's snoring. Once downstairs she took the five pounds from Eluned's purse and took one last look at the kitchen. Pádraig had left ten minutes earlier. The bus was due in five. She opened the door and closed it behind her as quietly as she could.

"What are you doing girl? Look at you, all dressed up!"

"I'm coming with you."

"What?"

She had wanted him to be happier. Now she suddenly felt the cold. Pádraig led her away from the bus stop. There was only one other person there, an austere looking woman in black.

"You have to stay," said Pádraig, his voice low and firm. His hands clasping her shoulders. "You can't come."

"But you said I should go. Go to the Fair City!"

"One day yes. But now now! Where will you stay?"

"I don't know! I thought... maybe..."

Pádraig sighed as he saw the tears.

"Here. Take this."

The handkerchief smelled of him. She dabbed her cheeks. The bus appeared in the distance and the austere woman in black picked up her bags in preparation. Miriam knew it was hopeless.

"Go back," said Pádraig. He squeezed both her arms and smiled sadly. "Really. I'll be back before you know it and, anyway, I'll write."

He kissed her on her cheek. Then he picked up his suitcase and stepped onto the bus. The doors closed behind him and the driver pulled off before Pádraig had even had a chance to sit down.

THREE

She fell backwards onto her handbag and she could feel and hear the plastic crunch of things breaking and snapping. Her make-up and lipstick. Her mirror. The driver shot out of the car and started to shout. There was a cigarette glued to the corner of his mouth

"What the hell were you thinking?"

Miriam sat up. The tarmac was rough against her palms. The young driver flicked away his fag and helped her up.

"I'm so sorry. I wasn't looking."

"Thank God *one* of us was!"

A small crowd had gathered to see if there was any blood or carnage and now they drifted away slowly, almost disappointed that the young girl who had been knocked down seemed to be okay apart from a dirty coat and a shattered bag.

"I hope I didn't damage your car."

The young man laughed.

"I was barely out of first gear. And anyway, I can't see how something as skinny as you could damage a Ford Popular."

She half smiled and walked away, trying hard to bury her face in her coat. Some of the people in the crowd on Caernarfon's main square – the Maes – must have recognised her as the young assistant from Mr Oliver's shoe shop. How she wished she lived in a big city where she could melt into the crowds and be anonymous whenever she felt like it. Somewhere like London or Liverpool. Or Dublin.

As she walked, patting down her coat and fluffing up her hair, she wondered what Pádraig was doing right at that moment. Had he been around he would have rowed with that man with the black Ford Popular. He might even have punched him on the nose. But then if Pádraig had been there she wouldn't have been run over in the first place. He was the reason why she'd stepped out without looking. She was thinking of him. Missing him. Wondering if she'd been forgotten and if there was another girl on the scene. Some Irish coleen. That's what he called the Irish girls back home. 'Coleens'. She'd always found it such a lovely word in the past but now it sounded ominous and threatening – like an Irish word for 'witch'.

"You're late."

"I know Mr Oliver. I'm sorry."

"Second time this week."

"It won't happen again."

He grunted and coiled the silver watch-chain into his waist-coat.

"Last warning. Do you understand?"

Mr Oliver smiled politely at Mrs Bennett and Mrs Bennett smiled back. Leah raised her eyebrows at Miriam but then, feeling the glare of Mr Oliver, she took out a shoe from a box and placed it in front of the customer.

"Try this one Mrs Bennett."

"Remember to lock up Leah."

"I will Mr Oliver."

"Dental appointment," said Mr Oliver, feeling that he owed his customer an explanation. "Two fillings."

"Oh dear," said Mrs Bennett.

"Can't be helped. Right. I'll bid you good day." He doffed his bowler hat in Mrs Bennett's direction. "See you tomorrow girls. Bright and early."

"Yes Mr Oliver."

Mr Oliver yanked down his cuffs, tightened his cravat and opened the door. The bell tinkled, there was a fleeting rush of cold air. And then he was gone.

Mrs Bennett shivered.

"Bit of a tyrant isn't he?" she said. "Gives me the creeps he does. I don't know how you can stand it. I see his wife in Woolworths sometimes. Meek as a mouse she is." She lowered her voice. "They say he beats her."

"Not too tight are they Mrs Bennett?" asked Leah.

"No love."

"Why don't you have a little walk round to check."

Mrs Bennett teetered across the carpet as if she was on a tightrope.

"I'll take them."

"I'll get the box."

At the end of the afternoon Leah locked up the shop as instructed. She even rattled the doors to double-check that they were secure.

"There," she said, dropping the keys in her handbag. "Even Harry Houdini couldn't get in now!"

FOUR

"I mustn't stay long," said Miriam. "My Dad would give me a real talking to if he knew I was coming in to The Britannia straight after work."

"You're with me," said Leah, teasingly. "I'll keep you on the straight and narrow. Mind you," she glanced over Miriam's shoulder and leant in, lowering her voice. "There's a man at the next table who keeps looking at you."

"At *me?*"

Leah whipped out her arm to stop Miriam from turning round.

"He's coming over."

"Oh God!"

"Just look calm. Sip your gin. Pretend you don't care."

"Mind if I join you?"

Leah looked up and flashed the stranger her best smile.

"Please do."

The stranger placed his pint on the table and sat down. His eyes were on Miriam all the time.

"No hard feelings I hope?"

"No," said Miriam, reddening. "Of course not."

Leah leant forward.

"What's going on?"

"We had a bit of a mishap," said the stranger. "She ran out into the road this lunchtime and I knocked her down."

"*What?*"

"Nothing," said Miriam, embarrassed and not wanting a fuss.

"Honestly Leah. It was my fault."

"Daniel," said the stranger, extending his hand to Leah. "Pleased to meet you."

Leah looked at the proferred hand with distaste. But, after a quick glance at Miriam, she took it.

"Let me get you girls another," said Daniel. "Same again?"

Pádraig's letters landed heavily on the porch mat twice a week. Sometimes there were photographs of Dublin inside, or pressed flowers plucked from Iveagh gardens – their delicate petals soft and almost translucent. His letters told her everything he'd been up to. His mother was on the mend and should be on her feet soon. Then he would come back to Wales. He told her not to worry.

But then there was another letter. The handwriting was unfamiliar and yet the postmark was local. Caernarfon. Eluned had propped it up against the marmalade jar one morning and the clear invitation was for Miriam to open it over the breakfast table but she just looked at it and tucked it in her pocket.

"It's not from Ireland," said Alwyn, winking mischievously at Eluned.

Miriam stood up.

"I'm late."

As the bus to Caernarfon rattled and rocked like a galleon, Miriam took the strange, thin letter out of her pocket and opened it. It wasn't a proper letter at all. It was a poem. Eight lines long, it seemed to describe mountains, skies and birds. She wasn't sure if she understood it. The Welsh it used was so dense, not the normal Welsh everyone spoke in Caernarfon and Pantglyn – this was more like the type of Welsh she'd had to learn in those boring old books at school. She turned the paper round just in case there had been anything written on the back but there wasn't. Strangely disappointed, she slipped the poem back in the envelope.

That afternoon Daniel came into the shop wearing a smart blue suit and with his thick black hair greased back in a shiny pile. It was Leah's afternoon off and Miriam was on her own.

"What are you doing here?"

"I need shoes."

He raised his foot.

"They seem fine to me."

"They pinch."

Mr Oliver cleared his throat in the back office.

"Sit down."

Daniel smiled and did as he was told. He took off his left shoe.

"Size ten," he said. "Preferably black. Nothing too fancy or expensive. And something I can wear to chapel."

He wasn't interested in new shoes. She wasn't born yesterday. She picked up a black leather brogue.

"How about something like this?"

Daniel didn't even look at it.

"Perfect."

"Try it on."

"Can you help?"

Miriam knelt down and gently guided his left foot into the brogue.

"You've got soft hands."

"Not too tight?"

"I'll take them."

"I'll fetch the box."

"Wait. Have you heard of T.J. Watcyn?"

"Who?"

"The great Bard. He's got one of those big old Victorian houses up in Twthill. He wrote a beautiful poem about the Spring and how it encourages lovers."

"I don't really read a lot of poetry. Let me get the box – "

"Hang on."

Daniel took her arm.

"He's giving a talk and a reading. Over at the Wilson Club on Saturday. I was wondering if you'd like to come."

"*Me?*"

"Why not?"

"But the Wilson Club is full of stuffy old men! Why would I want to go there?"

FIVE

She was the only woman in the room. A semi-circle of chairs curled around a lectern. Daniel leant over.

"Strange first date."

"It's *not* a date."

Guilt clenched up like a tiny fist inside her as she thought again of the two unanswered letters from Ireland tucked into the drawer of her dressing table at home. She still loved him. She knew that. They were virtually engaged after all. She was still going to go to Dublin, become a Catholic and have lots and lots of children. Pádraig would come back soon and take him with her as his wife next time he went.

A sudden burst of enthusiastic applause signalled the appearance of an old man in a brown jacket who stepped up to the lectern and placed a big black book in front of him like a minister about to unleash a sermon. His hair was long, much longer than any man's hair Miriam had ever seen and it was as white as woven cobwebs in sunlight. A young man placed a glass of whisky on the lectern next to the big black book and the old Bard looked surprised, but happy to see it. He raised it to the audience, took a sip and cleared his throat. The room became silent. Expectant. Daniel took her hand. Miriam thought of pulling it away but she didn't.

During a gap between the third or fourth poem – none of which Miriam had felt she understood – whilst T.J. Watcyn sipped his second whiskey, Daniel leant across to Miriam.

"He runs weekly classes here every Wednesday night," he whispered. "I'm thinking of going along. Introduce myself. Maybe take some of my poems for him to see."

"You should."

"He has his cronies though."

He nodded in the direction of a table near the lectern where three serious-looking young men were sitting down and taking notes. They were the ones who had bought T.J. Watcyn the whiskies.

"They're so much more advanced than me," said Daniel. "Older too. One of them has a beard!"

"You have to start somewhere," said Miriam. "And you can always grow a beard by Wednesday if you work at it."

Pádraig described a trip he'd taken to a bird sanctuary near the coast at Kilcoole. He'd even made some drawings in coloured pencils. One day, he wrote, he would love to live in a cottage by the sea. Preferably high up on a cliff. They could walk the pathways with their children and tell them all kinds of stories about Kings and Queens and mythical beasts. If he was concerned about her lack of replies he didn't mention it.

" *'Dear Pádraig,'* " she wrote one night. " *'Sorry I've been so slow in writing back. It's just that work has been so busy and Mr Oliver has been a right pain in the neck!'* "

She had never written a lie before.

" *'I wish I could find another job. I really do. Maybe when I come over to Dublin I can find something nice. In an office maybe. Typing or keeping things tidy.'* "

But Dublin had slipped away. Further than China.

" *'The bird sanctuary sounds nice. And such lovely drawings. How I wish I could draw. But I was always useless. All I could do were little stick men! The cottage by the sea sounds so lovely. Let's hope we can do that one day.'"*

She scribbled some crosses at the bottom of the page and a splash of perfume. Then she scrunched the paper up and threw it into the basket with all the others.

Two days later Daniel drove her out in the black Ford Popular and took her to the shores of Llyn Cwellyn, the deepest body of water in the county and reputed to be bottomless. A month later she discovered she was pregnant.

Nine months and a week later I arrived.

SIX

"More tea dear?"

"No thanks," said Miriam, sitting up and offering the old lady her best, most polite smile. The one she used on customers when she really wasn't in the mood. "I'm fine."

"You've hardly touched your food."

Miriam glanced down at her plate. Irish stew. Before she was a Meredith, Gladys had been a Morgan and everyone in Bethel had known that the Morgans were the only family for miles with their own cook. It was delicious. But Miriam couldn't eat a thing.

"You're eating for two now my dear."

The thing growing inside her was some sort of machine that she had no control over. Tiny bones and flesh folding into place all by themselves. It had invaded her body. Soon it would take over. And then it would want to break out. She put down her spoon.

There must have been tears in her eyes but she was determined not to cry. This was a house of appearances. Gladys Meredith was not the kind of woman who responded well to hysterics of any kind.

"I need to use the bathroom Mrs Meredith."

"Of course dear."

Miriam folded up her napkin as best she could – she had never been taught how – and excused herself. Daniel nodded and gave her one of his supportive, tight-lipped smiles but offered no words of comfort. At table with his mother he always reminded her of a little boy.

"Do you want more stew Daniel? There's some meat here."

"Just a spoonful, yes."

Gladys Meredith gave the signal and Beti served second-helpings to Daniel with a silver ladle. Miriam left the room and walked up the wide stairway.

She hadn't needed the bathroom at all. She had wanted to see her room. Nothing had been said yet but Daniel had said that he would ask his mother whether they could move in with her into Llys Meifor once the baby was born. Until they got settled. Daniel planned to go to college. Become a teacher. It wasn't as if lack of space would be an issue. Gladys now only used one of the six bedrooms.

Could she live in Llys Meifor?

The landing was enormous. Like the deck of a ship. The whole house felt as if it was full of ghosts. Shadows flickered everywhere across dark, polished wooden panels and Miriam's whole body was coiled tightly in expectation of some sudden manifestation. The howling wind didn't help. The whole house was surrounded by a pack of coyotes.

Could she live in Llys Meifor?

Daniel had described the room to her – the one that would be theirs – but this was the first time she'd seen it. She stepped in. A wardrobe in the far corner stood as still as a sentry. By the far window there was a large dressing table. Miriam walked over and picked up a photograph of a middle aged man in a waistcoat. He didn't look happy to be photographed. Miriam knew this was John Meredith, Daniel's father who had died ten years earlier. She replaced it. Next to his photograph there were a pair of braces and some neatly-folded ties. A dark shape made her catch her breath but then she realised it was only a suit hanging up on the wall just waiting to be picked up and worn.

This was where her baby would live. Here with Daniel. Here

with Gladys Meredith.
    And here with John.
    Could she live in Llys Meifor?
    What choice did she have?

SEVEN

"When you die, an angel takes you from your coffin and leads you to a long staircase which comes down from the clouds. At the top of these moving stairs there's a man called St Peter and he's got a very big book in front of him with the names of everybody who's supposed to come up that day."

"Why has he got names in there Nain?"

"Because he's been watching to see if you've been good."

"Like Santa?"

"St Peter is far more important. St Peter decides if you've been good enough to go through the big iron gates to heaven."

"What do the gates look like?"

"Very tall and heavy. They're made of iron and painted black."

"But wouldn't they fall through the clouds and come crashing down?"

I embellished my question with a descending whistle followed by my best explosion noise and described a circle of smoke with my arms.

"They don't fall through," said Nain.

Maybe things were different in heaven. Maybe after we died the laws of physics and gravity didn't apply. If anybody knew about these things Nain did. She read her Bible every day.

"What's heaven like Nain?"

I sat forward with my head in my hands. Nain smiled and thought about it.

"Well, I want you to close your eyes and imagine the most

beautiful place you've ever seen."

I closed my eyes tightly. I thought of the Marine Lake funfair in Rhyl.

"Are you imagining it?"

I nodded as hard as I could.

"Good. What can you see?"

"A roller-coaster."

"Well, there aren't any of those in heaven. Heaven is full of peace and quiet. It's where God lives."

"Does God have a house?"

"Of course."

"Does it have stairs and a toilet and a fridge and stuff?"

"I don't know about that."

"But he must have a fridge to keep his milk in and to make sure that nothing goes off."

I sensed that Nain was getting annoyed by all the questions about fridges.

"Everything that's important down here," she said, "is not considered very important at all in heaven. Not fridges or television or pop music or anything like that. Heaven is about salvation. It's about being at peace with God. If you're good and if you go to chapel and to Sunday School and if you do what you're told like your Dad did when he was a little boy and if you behave and devote more time to reading your Bible then maybe you will get to heaven one day."

"But I'd have to die first."

"We all have to die."

"I don't want to."

"There's nothing to be scared of," said Nain, making me jump when her hand touched mine. "If you've been good then it will all be fine."

But I wasn't good. I hardly spent any time reading the Bible. Nain had given me a brand new one for Christmas and, although I had flicked through it to try to find any exciting bits I had given up pretty quickly in favour of the *TV Tornado* annual which Santa had stuffed into my stocking. I was bad in other ways too. I picked my nose in chapel and wiped balls of snot under the pew.

"What counts as being bad Nain?"

"Stealing. Lying. Swearing. Taking the Lord's name in vain. Not doing what one is told. Refusing to eat Beti's carrots."

"Burping?"

"Burping always goes in the book."

I had refused to eat carrots hundreds of times. I shoved them to the corner of my plate every Sunday and squashed them with my knife to make them look smaller so that no one would notice. But St Peter had probably noticed. He had X-Ray eyes. And I burped all the time. I only said 'excuse me' when my Mum nudged me under the table with her foot. I wondered if St Peter had heard me when I'd said 'fuck' after dropping a shilling down a drain? He probably had X-Ray ears too.

"I'll never get to heaven."

"Then you must pray. Pray to God and he will hear you. He will tell Jesus. Then Jesus will tell St Peter."

"Heaven must be a pretty special place if everyone wants to go there so much."

Nain sighed and I opened my eyes. She was glancing across at the photograph of my Taid on the mantelpiece. John Meredith. The Taid I'd never known.

"It must be," she said. "Because when me and your Taid were very young he promised me that, if he died first out of the two of us, he would come back and tell me what heaven was like. When he did die and after they'd buried him in Llanddeiniolen cemetery

I waited for him night after night, looking up to the stars. But he never did keep his promise. It was the only time he didn't. So yes. Heaven must be really special."

EIGHT

John Meredith could slice slate as thin as paper. At the quarry he told the fresh crop of young apprentices who crowded around him every September that all they needed to do was find the sweet spot. Because a piece of slate was almost like a living thing. He would ask the boys if they'd ever stroked a cat. Some of them looked at each other with uncertainty. The braver ones would mumble that they had. So John Meredith explained that a cat always responded to a human hand and would guide it towards the spot where it wanted to be touched. The same was true of slate.

"Look at this mountain", he'd say, directing their confused but eager faces to the massive whale of rock that they were precariously balanced upon. "What we're doing is ripping this beautiful material out of Mount Orwig's belly. Newly-mined slate rumbles past us on these trains and trucks – huge slabs. Raw. Listen to the groaning and squealing of the metal wheels. That tells you how heavy it is. You'd think it was cold and unfeeling wouldn't you? But slate is alive boys. Trust me. As alive as you or me."

It was a well-rehearsed lecture, delivered every year and honed, by now, as perfectly as one of his slices of slate. These were the less sturdy boys. The ones who had been deemed unsuitable for face-work. They'd been sent over by Mr MacNamara to learn how to cleave slate into thin slices using only a mallet and chisel and John Meredith was the best they had. A true artist. Now he was telling them about cats and saying that slate was alive. He knew they probably thought he was a bit mad.

"Okay boys," he'd say, sticking the rolled-up cigarette behind his ear, "see how I'm tapping away at the rock with the blade of the chisel? What I'm searching for is that sweet spot. The place where, with one sharp tap of the mallet, the slate can be split cleanly and perfectly. That sweet spot is very important boys. It's the key that opens up the treasure. But like with a new cat, it takes a while to find it. Unlike with a cat however, with slate you only get one chance. Get it wrong and you blow it. Which is why it's important that you get it right. Otherwise all the men in Orwig – the men down in its bowels risking life and limb every day – won't be happy with you. The last thing they want to see is their hard work wasted."

He tapped the wooden hilt of the chisel. The blue-grey rock surrendered into two swooning squares.

"See how they're both the same thickness boys? Pass them round. They've both got to be exactly the same thickness otherwise they're no good."

The apprentices would all look at each other anxiously but, in time, most of them got the hang of it. Mr MacNamara always congratulated him on training up a new generation of skilled craftsmen and if he only knew how valuable he really was, Mr MacNamara thought, he could probably demand double his wages.

Singing was John Meredith's true passion. Twice in Bethel chapel of a Sunday the master cleaver's clear tenor voice would echo around the walls, swirling and soaring until it sounded in harmony with itself. Many suggested to him that he should enter an eisteddfod – some even suggested he may have been good enough to compete for the famed Blue Ribbon at the National Eisteddfod – but John Meredith would always politely brush them away. He only sang in chapel, he said. Singing for any other reason seemed wrong.

NINE

At first, the girl in the pew three rows back thought she was hearing an angel. Gladys had nodded off into a semi-conscious doze during a particularly tedious prayer by Dr Ffrancon-Rees and she had been transported to heaven where a beautiful and ethereal voice was enveloping her. It was only when her sister Kate nudged her that she woke up and realised that the prayer was over. The congregation was halfway through the first verse of the next hymn. Gladys shot to her feet, straightened her bonnet and opened her hymn book in the hope that it would magically find the right page. She daren't look across at her mother in case she'd been discovered. Dozing off in chapel! What would everyone say? What would Dr Ffrancon-Rees say? At least Kate seemed to think it was funny. Three pews in front of her she realised that the voice she had heard towards the end of her dream was not that of an imaginary angel at all. It belonged to a young man in a smart grey suit. All she saw was the back of his head. But it was enough to tell her that she was in love.

Anyone in Bethel who'd been told that one of the Morgan sisters was courting would probably have assumed that it was Kate. She was the pretty one. Brainy too. The first girl to enter Bangor University and gain a degree. It had even been in the *Caernarfon and Denbigh Herald* a few months earlier together with a photograph of her with her proud parents, Dr Idwal and Mary Morgan. But it was her shy and somewhat intense sister who found love first, and this surprised Gladys just as much as anyone else.

Dr Francon-Rees spoke of love whenever he came to Llys Meifor for tea. Mrs Morgan would have instructed Beti to lay out the finest cups and saucers in the front room and now, after a few slices of battenburg and some idle scraps of gossip, the maid was signalled to clear the table which she did with silence and ease. Once she had gone Dr Ffrancon-Rees would push back his chair, close his eyes and expound on a few key passages in the Holy Book, praying that another war could be avoided with Germany. Idwal would usually be in the surgery at the left wing of the house with a patient and Kate was often away in Bangor but Gladys was always there and she remembered the word 'love' being spoken by Dr Ffrancon-Rees almost like some form of incantation. From his dry, thin and corpse-like lips the word sounded different. The 'love' he spoke of wasn't the same kind of 'love' that Bing Crosby sang about or James Stewart punched people for on the huge screen at Caernarfon's Majestic cinema. This was a higher kind of emotion, something untainted by physical expression. God, said Dr Ffrancon-Rees, had created the world and had sacrificed his own son just in order to prove his love for us and to promise us the chance of eternal life. Surely, he'd say, there could be no purer love than that. But the love Gladys suddenly felt was different. Closing her eyes she saw the back of his head. The young man in the smart grey suit. She heard his voice.

The following Sunday she was up early for chapel and flicking through her wardrobe trying to find a dress that wasn't too showy but wasn't likely to make her vanish into the crowd either. She chose the blue one which her mother had bought her from Polecoff's in Bangor the previous Christmas. Dabbing some perfume behind her ear she adjusted her dress in front of the mirror to smooth out the creases before carefully placing the black hat on her head like a crown, tilted slightly.

"Looking very smart today Gladys."

"Thank you Dr Ffrancon-Rees."

"Not that you're not smart *every* Sunday of course!"

Gladys smiled politely. Beside her, Kate giggled. It was after the service and the congregation was milling out into the street outside Bethel chapel. Kate nudged her sister as John Meredith brushed past and Gladys tried not to blush. She saw him walking up to some of his friends from Orwig Quarry. All of them were in their best suits and holding shiny black hymn books. She couldn't hear what they were saying because Dr Ffrancon-Rees was talking to her mother about something to do with raising funds for the chapel roof but when one of the quarrymen finished one of his stories there was a loud burst of laughter. Gladys shot a glance across at them and saw her singing angel pop a Woodbine in his mouth. He checked his watch, placed an arm on the shoulder of one of his mates and winked. He was clearly telling them he had to go. As he went Gladys felt her heart protesting. If she didn't say something that very instant she would have to wait for another week. And she'd put on her blue dress specially.

"I enjoyed your singing."

Her voice sounded small, almost as if it belonged to someone else. In the silence after her words it felt as if the world had stopped. She couldn't even hear the birds in the trees. John Meredith turned to face her. He seemed surprised.

"Oh. Thank you."

He whipped the unlit Woodbine from his mouth.

"It's a lovely day," said Gladys, hoping he wouldn't notice the quake in her voice. Then she became aware of Kate standing beside her.

"My sister won't stop going on about your singing."

"Really?"

"Oh yes," said Kate. "She says you've got the voice of an angel."

John Meredith looked uncomfortable.

"I don't know about that."

"Do you like rabbit stew?"

"Stew?"

"Yes," said Kate. "Our maid Beti is probably the finest cook in Bethel and her rabbit stew is the stuff of legends. Next Wednesday Mr Meredith. Shall we say seven o'clock at Llys Meifor? I'll get Beti to lay out an extra place at table."

TEN

A white wedding had naturally been out of the question. Not with such a visible bump. And a ceremony at Bethel chapel was impossible too, Gladys had been quite clear about that. There was no way poor old Dr Ffrancon-Rees could have dignified such a charade.

"I'm more than happy to go through with it you know Gladys," said Dr Ffrancon-Rees, placing his china cup rather shakily on the table in Llys Meifor's front room. "I wouldn't want you to think that there was any kind of formal resistance from myself or the deacons."

Gladys pursed her lips.

"It won't happen at Bethel."

Dr Ffrancon-Rees was in his late eighties by now. Wispy hair hung over his ears and the children of Bethel weren't scared of him anymore. If anything they made fun of him behind his back. So few of them went to chapel now. Gladys blamed the cinema and the incomers to the new council estate. The new decade was just around the corner and the world was changing but clearly not for the better. Russia and America were at each other's throats and chapel seemed irrelevant in the face of imminent destruction.

"We can't let these unfortunate events stand in the way of Daniel and this young girl's happiness Gladys."

"A child born out of wedlock Dr Rees. You've always been very firm on these matters in the past."

"Well yes..."

Gladys rang the little bell. It was a signal that the discussion was at an end.

"So where will the wedding take place?" asked Dr Ffrancon-Rees.

"We've come to an arrangement. Me and the girl's family. The ceremony will be in Cysegr chapel in Pantglyn, the girl's village. Their minister will conduct the service and it will be a low-key affair. Both the girl's family and myself agreed that we didn't want a fuss."

Beti entered the front room as silently as a shadow and tidied up the plates and cups.

"And what is her family like Gladys?"

"The mother used to be a nurse so I believe. A matron in a hospital in Manchester before returning to Wales. I think she finds this whole situation as uncomfortable as we do."

"And what about the father?"

"A drunkard by all accounts."

"Oh dear."

"The girl is confused. I understand that she was thinking of converting to Catholicism less than a year ago because of some boy or other that she'd taken a fancy to. It doesn't bode well does it? That kind of flightiness? But Daniel is determined to go through with it. Doing the decent thing he says. He says he loves her."

Beti left the room. Gladys sighed heavily and glanced at a picture of John Meredith on the mantelpiece.

"It couldn't have happened at a worse possible moment," she said. "Daniel was about to arrange to go to college. Now he'll have to carry on in that council job in order to put food on the table. And they'll be living here for the time being of course. Where else can they go?"

"Poor Daniel," said Dr Ffrancon-Rees. "You know, I often

wonder what would have become of him at Preston North End."

He sat forward and placed his hand gently on Gladys's knee.

"People expect answers," he said. "And they expect them of me more than anyone. But I can't provide answers. Sometimes all I can do is point people in the direction of the right questions. Who knows? Perhaps if we asked the right questions then we might understand the answers."

ELEVEN

The wedding took place six weeks later on a chilly Saturday in March. If anyone had asked Miriam what Mr Eugene Lloyd, the minister, had said to her in his blessing then she wouldn't have remembered and she doubted if her new husband – standing as stiff as a grenadier guard beside her – would have either. Something about love no doubt. But this wasn't love. This wasn't how it was supposed to be. She wasn't supposed to feel like she wanted to cry. She could feel the baby squirming inside her as the minister droned on and on and on. It was as if it wanted to get out of there too. Out of the range of prying and judgmental eyes that were behind her and above her. Out of Pantglyn. Out of the county. But that wasn't going to happen. The writhing creature inside her had tied a knot around her life. She should have hated it for killing her dreams but, despite everything, she loved it. At that moment she knew that it was the only thing she loved for certain.

All those people watching, each one of them grateful it wasn't them. Daniel took the ring from his best man – someone called 'Gwilym' who she had never met before – and pushed it onto her finger. It wouldn't fit properly and he had to try not to look as if he was forcing. She smiled at the minister as if nothing was wrong. Finally she had to repeat his words and say 'I do'. And that was that. They were married. She'd expected trumpets and angels. That's how she'd envisaged her wedding when she'd been a little girl. There would be choirs and dancing children and the whole of Pantglyn would be out with banners and balloons to cheer and to celebrate. But now all that happened was that everyone sang a mournful hymn and after that the minister shook her hand. The Gwilym man who she had never met before shook her hand too and pecked her on the cheek. He nodded at Daniel and after the ceremony she never saw him again.

Outside there was a photographer who herded them together as if he was in a hurry to go somewhere more exciting. The rain was icy and the wind was like a mischievous child lifting skirts and ruffling up hair. Miriam posed with Daniel holding a little bouquet of flowers like a prize at a funfair and she smiled as hard as she could. Daniel's face was frozen into a smile she couldn't read. Leah came up with a concerned face and asked her if she was warm enough. Her arms were bare, she said. She didn't want to catch pneumonia. She offered Miriam a cardigan but she refused it. This was her wedding day and there was no way she was going to wear a cardigan. Gladys leant forward to give her new daughter-in-law a dry kiss on the cheek.

The car was waiting. It was a Ford Anglia driven by a man in a suit who, when he saw them approaching, spat out his rollie and killed it with his heel as if it was a cockroach. He opened the door for her, but it was a two-door model and so he pulled the front seat forward to make room for her in the back. There was no need to gather in the long trail of a wedding dress because she was wearing a plain green outfit Eluned had bought her from Nelson's in Caernarfon. Eluned had asked for a larger size than usual.

Miriam looked out at the diminishing crowd outside the chapel as they smiled and waved, all of them desperate for the car to go so that they could return to their homes. The driver started the engine and the Ford Anglia pulled off. In the mirror, Miriam watched Pantglyn fall away like something suddenly cut loose.

They were going to pick up the suitcases to go on their honey-moon. Daniel had booked a weekend in London.

On the Saturday he took her to Stamford Bridge to see Chelsea play Arsenal.

TWELVE

He'd always been good at catching. Throw him a ball, John had said, and he'd get it every time. Uncle Myrddin, Kate's husband, had taken up the challenge on more than one occasion and he was no slouch when it came to throwing things. His arms were as tough as tyres and the manky old tennis ball was hurled like a bullet but, despite this, the ten year old Daniel never flinched. He never dropped a catch. Uncle Myrddin always laughed.

"That lad of yours is going to be a first class cricketer one day John."

But cricket wasn't the game. Cricket was too posh for north Wales. And there was too much gorseland. The stumps would have sunk before anyone could have hit them. In Bethel there was only one game and Daniel's room at the top of Llys Meifor was covered with pictures of Stanley Matthews.

"There'll be pictures of me in football magazines one day," he told his father. "I'll be just like Stanley Matthews and they'll all cheer my name."

Sadly, he couldn't kick. Faced with a goalscoring opportunity at the County School in Caernarfon he fluffed it. The ball either went flying over the bar or rolled harmlessly towards the nearest defender. At fifteen he realised that he wasn't special after all and that, like every other boy in the school, he would have to knuckle down to study hard for his exams in order to avoid the quarry or the local factory. But then one afternoon Mr Roe the sports teacher did with Daniel what he always did with the boys who were keen but fundamentally useless. He put him in goal. And that's where everything changed.

He was drawn to the ball. Whether it was kicked or headed towards him his hands instinctively found the spot to either catch it or punch it or tip it over the bar to safety. Speed didn't scare him. Strikers loved to intimidate by shouting or screaming at him as they charged into his box but Daniel always stood his ground and kept his eyes firmly on the ball, anticipating each shift in direction, realizing he only had a split second to react. Despite his smaller than usual frame he wasn't scared to come out either, to charge at the striker and force him wide so that the angles were reduced. He had an instinct to stop the ball that was as strong as a striker's instinct to move it and it only took a few games for Mr Roe to realise that he had a natural talent on his hands. By the time he was sixteen Daniel Meredith was not only playing for the School First XI, he was also the reserve goalkeeper for local team Caernarfon Town.

The Oval wasn't *the* Oval. This Oval was a rectangle. A scrap of land in the north of Caernarfon surrounded on three sides by concrete steps which were slowly being reclaimed by weeds and tufts of gorse. There was a grandstand but it was hardly worth the extra shilling to sit on a wooden bench in a brick shell covered by a rusty corrugated roof. The Oval was as intimidating as a Roman amphitheatre. From the terraces the Caernarfon fans hurled obscenities like spears. Players on opposing teams were seen to tremble as they went over to take a corner and visiting goalkeepers were pelted with pie crusts. The referees could offer only scant protection. In Caernarfon their whistles were as impotent as Westminster.

"Mr Conway wants me in the first team."

"And who's Mr Conway when he's at home?"

"The manager."

Daniel had expected the silence. He'd been dreading it. It was punctuated by the languorous clunk of the grandfather clock in the corner and the clack of cutlery round the table.

"Next Saturday," he continued, trying to adopt a cheerful and carefree tone. "Against Bangor. They're top of the league."

"I thought they already had a goalkeeper," said John.

"They do," said Daniel. "But Mr Conway has asked me to step in as first choice."

"What about your schooling?" asked Gladys, avoiding his eye. "You've got exams coming up."

"I know."

"Mr Harris told me that some more of your poems were in the school magazine this term."

"Yes."

"It's your choice," said Gladys, avoiding his eye again and reaching for more carrots. "We won't force you. If you want to throw your life away on a stupid game then that's your affair."

THIRTEEN

A few weeks later Gerry Conway came up to Daniel after a match and led him away into a quiet area at the back of the grandstand. He lit a cigar.

"It's going well son."

"Yes Mr Conway."

Was he about to be dropped? Why was Gerry Conway talking to him? And why was he smiling? Gerry Conway never smiled. Daniel noticed how brown his teeth were. Brown as chocolates.

"A few more results like the ones we've been having lately son and we can leave this poxy league and get into the Northern Premier."

The cigar smoke was rich and pungent. It made Daniel want to cough. His eyes began to run but he resisted the urge to rub them.

The Northern Premier. That was certainly a big dream. Hardly any clubs from north Wales had ever played in it. But Gerry Conway was a man with big dreams, everyone knew that. A brash Londoner who had left school at fifteen with no qualifications and − it was rumoured − an inability to read, he was completely unsuited to anything in life outside football or crime. Some uncharitable souls in The Castle pub had suggested that Gerry Conway saw little distinction between those worlds. His instructions to his defenders nearly always involved the use of physical violence. If an opposing attacker got past them they were to mow him down. Break his leg if they had to. If they got sent off then so be it. The way he saw it being in a team was like being in the army. You looked after your mates. Not that Gerry Conway had seen any action during the war. The same uncharitable souls in The Castle rumoured darkly that he had connections in Soho. People who could be very persuasive when it came to little things like conscription. People who could even cause Churchill to have second thoughts.

"I hear you're something of a poet."

"Well, I..."

"Most players are dumb as mules. They do one thing and that's it. And some of them can't even do that. But you're different Daniel."

It was the first time Gerry Conway had called him by his name. Usually it was 'you,' 'son' or 'fuckwit'. Something was definitely up. And Daniel began to feel uncomfortable.

"Is everything all right Mr Conway? You're happy with my form?"

Gerry Conway took the cigar out of his mouth. He slapped Daniel hard on the shoulder.

"Couldn't be happier son. You're the best goalkeeper we've ever had."

But then his hand slipped away and the smile vanished.

"And that's the fucking problem. They're sending Tommy Kildare over. You heard of Tommy Kildare son?"

"No Mr Conway."

The Londoner emitted a low growl.

"I knew him back at Arsenal. Could have been a great centre half but he snapped his ankle during a fourth round cup tie at Goodison and he was never the same after that. So he took to the bottle – usual story – until Preston North End took him on as a scout. And now he's coming here."

"To Caernarfon?"

"To the arse end of the fucking world. Just to see you."

"But..."

Gerry Conway clenched his fist and snarled.

"Fucking vultures. You try to keep something quiet but they always fucking find you."

"I don't understand Mr Conway. What happens now?"

Gerry Conway looked at Daniel.

"What happens now son is that Tommy swans up in his black fucking Daimler in time for next week's game and takes his seat in the grandstand. We give him a cup of shitty tea and a complimentary sandwich and, after the match, he has a word with me, I send for you, he shakes your hand and asks you a few dumb questions. Then he'll invite you over to Preston for a trial and if all goes well, you'll be offered terms and, who knows, in a couple of years you'll be picking up your FA Cup winner's medal only..." He leant in closer and lowered his voice. "It ain't gonna fucking happen."

"I..."

Gerry Conway leant in and growled like a bear.

"You're going to have a bad day. Understand? Next Saturday you're going to find that those hands of yours are suddenly made of paper. When they get a corner or a free kick and that ball comes towards you you're going to fuck it all up. You're going to make stupid mistakes. Not too many, we don't want to make it bleeding obvious. Just enough to let them get two or three goals that they shouldn't have had. Get my drift son?"

There must have been something about his young goalkeeper's innocence and earnestness that appealed to him because Gerry Conway smiled and laid his arm on his shoulder in a fatherly manner.

"Look son, nobody likes success more than me. I was one of those youngsters myself once. I was spotted and given a chance and I had a good run. Nothing spectacular, I didn't get an FA Cup medal or anything like that but I scored some goals at Old Trafford and Stamford Bridge before the war came and fucked it all up. You're the brightest light we've got and you deserve better than this and, trust me, I'm going to help you get there. Only not yet, that's all."

He sighed.

"I'm too old to score goals now. But I'm young enough to get a second chance at the big time from the stand. I can put teams together and get them to the top of the league. Maybe one day someone from one of the big teams is going to say that old Gerry Conway is playing a blinder at Caernarfon Town and they're going to come calling with a nice offer. But for that to happen I need a strong team. And I can't afford to lose my star players. So, next Saturday, do me a favour eh son? Send that bastard vulture back to Preston thinking you're no better than a part-time butcher or postman. Then, as soon as we've won this poxy league I promise you I'll put in a call to some people I know and I'll make sure you get a trial with one of the big clubs. Have we got a deal son? We going to shake on it?"

He held out his hand. Daniel shook it.

Whether it was the cigar smell or the deal, as soon as Gerry Conway was gone he ran out into the patch of rough ground and threw up.

FOURTEEN

Dreams were the privilege of the idle rich. Whilst the well off could afford the time to ponder life's possibilities and the various routes that it might take, for the likes of John Meredith those routes had been carved in slate ever since he'd been a young boy. He would work in Orwig Quarry just as his father had done and as his grandfather had done before him. At least John had been luckier than most. His slight frame had counted against him when it came to working underground and his uncanny talent for cleaving slate had been spotted by one of the foremen. So while his old schoolmates stuffed themselves into tight tunnels a mile or more beneath him and coughed out their lungs every evening until, by the time they were thirty, they could hardly reach the end of a sentence without stopping for breath, John could sit with his chisel and his hammer slicing slate into perfect sheets and breathe in the cold Eryri air. True, he had to work outside in all weathers – even when it snowed – but he considered himself lucky. His talented hands had saved him from the very pits of Hell. And now he was in love. He saw her face in the pieces of slate he cleaved. He heard her voice in the whistle of the quarry train that took him home. He saw her shape in the puffs of steam. He was in love with someone he had never actually spoken to. Someone he had only seen from a distance in Bethel chapel. Three pews apart might as well have been three million miles. He was in love with Gladys Morgan. It was impossible.

One evening after supper, John Meredith was about to go

upstairs to re-heel his boots when his father laid an arm on his shoulder and invited him out into the back garden for a talk. Both men sat down on a plank of wood supported by three rusty barrels. John was offered a cigarette. Puzzled, he took one. His father lit it. Then he lit his own, inhaled deeply, picked out a sprig of tobacco from the tip of his tongue and flicked it into the night.

"Twenty one," said his father. "Seems only yesterday you were a boy in short pants."

John smiled. It seemed the only appropriate response. In the distance, Mount Orwig loomed like the back of a surfacing kraken. Behind it lay Snowdon itself. Untainted and unmined. Black as a barren planet.

"I was talking about you to Meirion Lewis the other day."

Why would his father be talking about him to Meirion Lewis?

"Oh?"

"He's a fine man."

John Meredith pulled on his cigarette. Meirion Lewis was a fool and a lazy one at that. Whenever there was any hard work to be done at the quarry Meirion Lewis was always the shirker. Always the one with an excuse. People knew not to trust Meirion Lewis. His father knew it. So why was he talking like this?

"His eldest is growing up to be a handsome young woman."

"I hadn't really noticed," said John Meredith, suddenly realizing where this was going.

"Delyth's quite a beauty."

"I've got to go and see to my boots."

He stood up but so did his father blocked his path.

"I can see it."

"What?"

"Don't come the innocent with me boy! I wasn't bloody born yesterday!"

Realizing he'd raised his voice he looked anxiously back into the house and lowered it to a spit-filled whisper.

"I know what's going on and so does your mother. And it won't be long before the whole of the village does. Then we'll be a bloody laughing stock. Is that what you want?"

"I don't know what you mean."

"That Morgan girl. I've seen the way you look at her."

His father sighed. He stared at his son for a few seconds. Looked away. Looked at his cigarette. Flicked it away as if he was surprised to see it. Looked back at the house. Then at his son.

"She's the daughter of a doctor."

"I know."

"So what the hell are you thinking of? They live in that bloody big house – they've even got a *cook* for God's sake!"

He was trying to control his frustration but the spit was spraying warmly onto John's cheeks.

"It can't happen. Do you get that boy?"

"Yes Dad."

"It can't bloody happen!"

FIFTEEN

Llys Meifor had once been much grander, Miriam could see that. But it was still a handsome and distinguished house, by far the biggest in Bethel, set apart from the terraced streets by a spacious walled garden at the front and back. The two bay windows on the ground floor bulged forwards like the eyes of a giant toad and the patio with a rusty swing settee reminded her a little of those old-fashioned mansions she'd seen in *Gone with the Wind*. In her rare moments of solitude Miriam liked to wander around the silent corridors imagining the house as it once was. Back when the village was isolated and untouched by the twentieth century. Before radio and the cinema. Before the main road had brought speeding cars, lorries and vans. Before the council estate on the other side of the gorse fields. Before the baby.

Wandering out into the large back garden she could see how, once, the overgrown and dishevelled orchard and the dark goldfish pond must have been an idyllic playground for Gladys and Kate when they were little girls and jealousy pricked her like a fly. She'd always wanted a garden like that when she'd been little. Llys Meifor was now her home, but not quite. Because sometimes Miriam would get up in the morning, cross the creaky landing and wonder why she was tip-toeing like a ballerina. She was family now. Gladys had a three month old grandson. Miriam had every right to be there and she needn't have to worry about advertising her presence. And yet when the baby started to cry she would hold it to her breast and urge him to be quiet in case he woke the old woman up. She rocked him back and forth and cried too – her tears dropping onto his head.

"It's just her way," whispered Daniel one night in bed. "You'll get used to it."

"I'm not sure if I want to."

"Well, you're going to have to. Until things settle. Until I get to college and do teacher training."

"But that could take years!"

"Keep your voice down!"

The door to their bedroom was half-open in case of the baby and Miriam had almost wanted Gladys to overhear her outburst from her grand bedroom across the landing. But then she regretted it.

"I'm sorry," she said, whispering again. She flopped back against the pillow and sighed. "I'll try."

A few days later it was sunny and Miriam spotted Gladys out in the back garden, her black robes rippling like the feathers of an enormous crow. Placing the sleeping baby in the cot and tucking him in Miriam ventured out. Gladys was struggling with a rake as she tried to clear dead leaves from the surface of the pond.

"Here," said Miriam, "let me help."

"I can manage."

Miriam had no idea how deep the pond was but Gladys was now leaning forwards precariously as she tried to reach some of the leaves in the middle. Miriam saw her wobble and feared that she might lose her balance.

"Let me."

As she wrenched the rake from her hands Gladys seemed momentarily shocked. Normally the girl was so timid. She watched as Miriam fished out the troublesome leaves and left them in a wet pile by the side of the pond. Picking off a few strays from the teeth, Miriam leant the rake against a tree. The sun was warmer than she'd thought. She was sweating.

"I did ask Daniel to do it," said Gladys. "But he never gets round to these things. Besides, he was scared of that pond ever since he was a little boy."

"Really?"

"His father used to tell him there were monsters at the bottom that would eat him if he got too close."

Miriam smiled.

"I must sit down," said Gladys, wincing and pinching her back.

She gathered up her black robes until it looked as if she was engulfed by a stormcloud and sat on the wooden bench. Miriam sat down beside her. The breeze ruffled the trees. Twittering birds spread unintelligible gossip.

"It's lovely here," said Miriam. "I would have loved a pond like this when I was a little girl."

Gladys nodded as if her daughter-in-law was a polite stranger at a bus stop. But Miriam was determined not to let the moment go. She wanted to make a connection. Half-turning, she saw the carved names on the back of the bench. Gladys and John in a ragged heart.

"Did he carve that for you? How lovely!"

Gladys suddenly stared at her, unmistakable fury in her eyes.

"I must go," she said, getting up and almost tripping over her unruly robes. "Dr Ffrancon-Rees is coming for tea." She stopped just before the path and turned round. "And your baby is crying again."

My baby. That's what she calls him. Never by his name. Not even *our* baby!"

She was whispering in bed again.

"Go to sleep."

Daniel turned over and pulled the sheet over his head but Miriam lay gazing around the room. At the wardrobe which told her to go. At the dressing table that told her to go. At the photograph of John Meredith that told her to go. At the chair that told her to go. At the window that told her to go. At the trees that told her to go. At the moon that told her to go.

Once she was sure that Daniel was asleep she began to cry.

SIXTEEN

The baby was ill. Miriam was no expert but after two days of his piercing hysterics she knew that this wasn't normal. His tiny face, usually so playful and so willing to be entertained by the nameless wonders of his new world, was now a series of agonized wrinkles and lines. No amount of rocking or lullabying would do the trick.

Was it her fault? Was it something she was doing wrong?

There was no one around to help. Daniel was out at work and Gladys, as ever, was as unapproachable as an iceberg. The doctor's surgery took place in the village hall every Tuesday and Friday afternoon between two and half-past four. It was Tuesday so Miriam checked the ponderous grandfather clock. Twenty past three. If she hurried she might just make it.

The baby didn't stop crying as she walked quickly down the street. He didn't stop crying as she passed Mrs Williams from next door to one and forgot to say hello. He didn't stop crying as she entered the back of the village hall. He didn't stop crying as she sat down at the end of the row of chairs. He didn't stop crying as she rocked him so as not to irritate the other people waiting. He didn't stop crying as they smiled at her and she tried to smile back. He didn't stop crying as her turn came. He didn't stop crying. He would never stop crying. Soon she was crying too.

The doctor was young. Not much older than her. He took the baby from her, checked his temperature, felt his little belly and then handed him back, warm as a freshly-baked loaf. Miraculously he had stopped crying and, somehow, had fallen asleep. The young doctor swung round to his desk and scribbled something out. Miriam tried to read his face.

Was there concern there? Was it something she should know about? Was it all her fault?

"Is he alright?"

The young doctor carried on scribbling.

"Yes. Nothing too much to worry about. A mild digestive issue. Perhaps he took something in that he shouldn't have. It happens sometimes. This should help."

He ripped off the piece of paper he'd been scribbling on and handed her a prescription for something she couldn't pronounce.

"What do you mean it happens *sometimes? What* happens sometimes? I don't understand."

The doctor sighed as if this was something he'd had to explain a thousand times, but he tried to be polite about it.

"Contamination," he said. "It's a lot more common than you'd think. And it can be anything. A spot of dirt on the spoon perhaps, something that wasn't scraped off properly. Just a tiny amount of bacteria can cause a reaction, especially in a young baby like this. Have you been making sure the spoons you use for his food are scrupulously clean?"

Miriam opened her mouth to say 'yes' but she realised that, for the past couple of days, she hadn't actually fed the baby at all. Gladys had insisted on doing it. This had struck her as being a little unusual and, at first, she'd been reluctant to allow it – although she couldn't express why, not even to herself – but in the end she'd handed him over. The baby had gurgled happily and Gladys had even smiled at him, poking her finger out gently and stroking the side of his soft cheeks. She assured Miriam that she knew what she was doing. She had raised a child of her own after all. Miriam had felt her entire body tensing up as if it was on a drawstring. Seeing her holding her precious baby in Gladys's arms felt weird. She was convinced she might drop him. She had visions of the baby's egg-like skull cracking. She wanted to reach out and snatch him back but she didn't dare.

"I wouldn't worry," said the young doctor gently. "And don't take it personally. It happened to me too with my child. Just make sure everything is clean and he'll be fine. In the meantime just give him a spoonful of that twice a day and it'll clear up in no time."

"Thank you doctor."

An hour or so after the visit to the surgery Miriam woke up with a start to find Gladys hovering over her. It was unusual for her to fall asleep during the afternoons and she felt guilty. She sat up on the sofa and looked over to the cot. It was empty. The baby was in Gladys's arms.

"He was awake," she said. "So I fed him. I hope you don't mind?"

Miriam sat up and ran her hand through her hair. She must have looked a mess and she hated looking a mess in front of Gladys. The baby started crying and Miriam held out her arms.

"Let me take him."

"He's too hot. He's got too many blankets."

"He hasn't got too many blankets. Let me take him. Give him to me!"

She'd said it too loudly and too forcefully. Daniel walked in from work and placed his briefcase on a chair.

"What's going on?"

"Nothing," snapped Miriam, sitting back and realizing that she had sounded like a sulky schoolgirl.

Gladys stroked the baby and smiled gently at Daniel.

"She's had a little rest," she said. "Poor thing was exhausted. So I just gave the baby a little feed. He's too hot though. Let me take him through to the pantry. It'll be cooler for him there."

"No!"

Miriam stood up and tried to snatch the baby away but Daniel stopped her. She watched helplessly as Gladys left the room with her baby in her arms.

"What the hell's the matter with you?" asked Daniel.

She heard Gladys go into the pantry. Bottles were moved. The baby was still crying. She felt like a failure.

Was this all her fault?

She buried her head in Daniel's chest and sobbed. It took a long time for his arm to comfort her. Far too long.

"You have to give her a chance," he said, whispering in bed again.

"A chance to what? Make the baby ill?"

"Don't be so ridiculous."

Miriam leant up to face him.

"The doctor said there was contamination. I've seen the way she feeds him. She uses the same rusty spoon and she only washes it quickly under the tap."

"Only last week you were complaining that she never made an effort. Now you're complaining because she *does!*"

"You're never here. You don't know!"

"She finds it hard," said Daniel. "After what happened with my father. This all brings it back. Just give her a chance."

SEVENTEEN

The sticky red stuff that the young doctor had prescribed appeared to have done the trick. After a couple of days, the baby stopped crying and his face became less tortured. Once again he smiled and gurgled with joy as Miriam poked his fat belly.

But shame swelled inside her like a bruise. She'd read articles in some of the trashy women's magazines about how first-time mothers sometimes developed irrational fears and suspicions. It was probably just that. Irrationality. Stupidity. Gladys had been kind in allowing them to move in to Llys Meifor until they found their feet – she had even cleared away a lot of the stuff that had belonged to John Meredith to make more room for the baby's nursery. Miriam was ungrateful and unreasonable to accuse her of not taking enough care with a stupid rusty spoon when, in all probability, all she had tried to do was help and create some kind of bond with her grandson.

Alone in Llys Meifor's dusty old library whilst Gladys entertained Dr Ffrancon-Rees on one of his weekly visits for tea, Miriam held the baby to her breast and resolved that, as soon as Dr Ffrancon-Rees had left, she would go into the front room and apologise for being so frosty and spiky. She would thank Gladys for all her help and kindness. She would even offer the baby for her to hold. As she held the baby to her breast however she could feel his temperature rising. Was his face getting redder? Was that drool on his face or sweat? Her first instincts were to take him outside into the back garden for a bit of fresh air but then she saw that it was beginning to rain so Miriam took him into the pantry instead.

It was one of the few rooms in Llys Meifor she hadn't been to – the place where Gladys made and stored her various jams, chutneys and piccalilli. It was as chilly as a tomb. She felt the baby's forehead but the coldness of her hand caused him to start sobbing. "I'm sorry," said Miriam. "We'll only stay a few minutes. Until you cool down."

She rocked him gently and looked up at the shelves all around her. How many jars of jams and chutney had Gladys produced over the years? Hundreds. Thousands. Neat, handwritten labels indicated strawberry jam, apricot, plum, damson. There must have been at least thirty jars of various shapes and sizes. With one hand, Miriam carefully dislodged a jar of damson jam from the shelf. She was about to inspect the label when she saw the rusty spoon behind it. It was the same one Gladys had used with the baby food. It was right next to a jar of rat poison.

Gladys was sitting on the bench by the goldfish pond. Hearing frantic feet on the path she turned round and saw Miriam, wild-eyed, baby in one hand, tin of rat poison and rusty spoon in the other.

"You took him into the pantry didn't you?" she said, barely able to control her voice as the anger shook her very bones. "You took him where no one could see you and you poisoned him! You're sick!" She dared to come closer. "Sick and *evil!*"

Breathless, she wanted to collapse and cry. The world was mad. The world was against her. And now Gladys had made it worse by just smiling. Then by laughing.

"*This is not funny!*" screamed Miriam.

Calmly, Gladys stood up and took the rat poison and spoon from Miriam's hand. She was still laughing as she flipped open the lid and dipped the spoon into the white powder. She was still laughing as she put it in her mouth. Still laughing after she'd swallowed it.

EIGHTEEN

As he took his seat in the grandstand at the Oval just as the referee blew his whistle for the kick-off, Tommy Kildare couldn't have been more conspicuous had he worn a clown outfit complete with spinning flower and size twenty-eight shoes. Regulars in the sparsely occupied grandstand had stood up and doffed their caps as if he'd been royalty as he'd made his way to his seat but Kildare had remained impassive. He sat down, studied the crudely-produced programme and, for one fleeting moment, he caught Daniel's eye. The young goalkeeper immediately looked away. He patted his gloves together and tried to focus on the game.

Caernarfon Town versus Pwllheli Wanderers. Hardly the stuff of dreams. This wasn't Goodison Park or Highbury. This was the windswept Oval where the gales from the Menai Straits were so strong that high-kicked balls were often suspended in the air for much longer than the laws of gravity were assumed to permit. It was a game that Caernarfon Town were expected to win, Pwllheli Wanderers were bottom of the table and had lost all their matches so far but, despite this, Daniel saw Gerry Conway standing on the touchline in front of his rusty, corrugated steel dug out, yelling at the defenders and waving his cigar around – shards of tobacco shooting off like sparks.

With less than a minute to go until half-time, and with the game still goalless, Pwllheli cleared a corner and a long ball found the feet of their lone centre forward, Huw Sarn. He was slower than most but what he lacked in speed he more than made up for in bullish power. He swept past the defenders and thundered towards Daniel's goal, the ball at his feet, nostrils flaring steam.

Daniel came out to the edge of his box and spread out his arms to make himself as big as he could as the Oval became as silent as a stone. He knew that, in reality, there were jeers and shouts from the crowd because, out of the corner of his vision he could see the waving arms and the scarves, but he blocked them out. All his ears heard were the thunderous hooves of Huw Sarn, his panting nose and the deep, leathery thud of the ball as it rocketed past him towards the top corner of the goal. Daniel watched it spin through the air almost in slow motion, the laces flapping, bits of mud and grass falling away. He saw his own hands reaching up, gloved fingers outstretching, rising like a bird – making contact.

In a flash the real world returned as his body thumped down into the stud-pocked mud. The ball had been tipped over the bar for a corner. But there was no time to take it because at that point the referee's whistle trilled for half-time.

Gerry Conway grabbed his young goalkeeper by the shoulder and marched him down the corridor into the smelly toilet which was supposed to be for the sole use of game officials but which had been out of order for months. The manager kicked down the seat and pushed Daniel onto it.

"What did I fucking say? No fucking heroics. I thought we had a deal."

"I couldn't help it Mr Conway."

Gerry Conway looked at him for a few seconds.

"Do me a favour eh son? You scratch my back, and I'll scratch yours. You understand?"

"Yes Mr Conway."

Daniel ran out to his new goal, performed a few athletic jumps to loosen up, touched the crossbar for luck and checked the grandstand. Tommy Kildare was back in his seat. He was holding a notebook and jotting something down.

The whistle went for the start of the second half and within five minutes Caernarfon Town were 2-0 up. Pwllheli Wanderers were a beaten side, but no one had told Huw Sarn. The big centre-forward broke away with a loose ball and closed in on Daniel's goal. No defender was close. It was going to be a straight duel between striker and goalie. Huw Sarn entered the box and prepared to shoot. Daniel dived for the ball but the angular and ungainly striker was more agile than he looked and he swerved expertly to avoid the challenge. Daniel's glove stroked his ankle and Huw Sarn collapsed into the mud, writhing and screaming as if he'd just been shot.

The referee whistled for a penalty.

Huw Sarn rose from the mud like Lazarus. He placed the ball on the muddied-out spot, took a few steps back, ran up and tucked the ball past the diving Daniel into the left corner as easily as if he was posting a letter. As he picked the ball up from the tangle of the net and booted it dejectedly towards the centre circle, Daniel looked across at Gerry Conway. The manager winked at him. Anyone who saw it might have interpreted it as a gesture of simple encouragement to a disappointed young goalkeeper but Daniel knew its true significance and now he felt dirty. Even when the rain began to spatter down it didn't help. All the rain in the world wouldn't have been enough to cleanse him.

NINETEEN

Daniel chucked the muddy kit into his bag, hitched it across his shoulder and got out of the dressing room without even bothering to change his boots. He rattled unsteadily down the corridor, past the stinking toilet and towards the exit which led out onto the rough patch of ground at the back of the Oval. But then he stopped. He saw the black Daimler parked next to an enormous grey puddle. Then, from behind, he heard a voice.

"You like it?"

He turned.

"Mr... Kildare!"

"A bugger to run," he said, nodding casually in the direction of his car. "Costs me a fortune in petrol. I'm thinking of getting something smaller to be honest. A Zephyr maybe. Or a Zodiac. Cigarette?"

Daniel shook his head.

"Very wise," said Kildare. "I'm thinking of giving these up too."

He lit the cigarette, shook the match and flicked it out through the door into a puddle where it fizzed faintly. As he blew out the smoke Daniel could see his eyes narrowing. He was studying the young goalkeeper like a scholar pondering a text.

"How old are you?"

"Sixteen. Almost seventeen."

"Got plans?"

Daniel shrugged and laughed nervously.

"Don't know really. Do my exams. Go to college if I can. Something like that. I don't know."

"I mean your real plans. Do you want to play football?"

"Well, yes."

"Ever been to Preston?"

Daniel shook his head. Swift as a magician, Tommy Kildare produced a card from his inside pocket. There was a phone number written on it neatly in blue ink.

"If you're serious about playing football then come to Preston a week Monday. Ring that number from the station and someone will pick you up. Bring your own boots and gloves. We'll provide the rest."

Daniel knew what the reaction would be and he wasn't looking forward to the row – especially from his mother. But he had to tell them. Finally, on the day before he was expected in Preston, he blurted it out as they were walking home from chapel.

"I've been offered a trial," he said. "With Preston North End."

Gladys stopped. It took a few seconds for the word to make sense.

"Preston?"

She said it as if it was on the other side of the world. Or on another planet. Daniel felt the hymn book sliding through his fingers because of the sweat.

"Tomorrow. And I'm going to go."

Gladys started walking again. Her pace was quicker than before. It was exactly the reaction he'd been dreading. He ran after her.

"It'll be fine," he said. "It's only a trial."

Gladys stopped.

"And what if they take you?"

Daniel was stuck. He looked at John for some kind of help and although he could see that his father was searching for the right words, nothing came out so Daniel turned to his mother again.

"I've got to try," he said. "Not everyone gets a chance. This man came all the way to see me last week."

"Last *week?*"

"I know. I should have said."

When Gladys walked away Daniel felt as if everything he'd ever known in the world had suddenly been pulled away from under his feet. The trees and bushes and houses all around him receded and all sounds faded away.

"Is she still angry with me?"

"She'll get over it."

Daniel sat next to his father on the bench overlooking the pond in Llys Meifor. Occasionally there was the plop of a fish as it broke the surface.

"Do you think it's wrong for me to go?"

John sat forward on the bench and sighed.

"Football's such a risk," he said. "You could break your leg in two weeks and what then? And there's so little money or security in it."

John looked him in the eye.

"But you're young. One day you'll be a teacher or a manager or heaven knows what – you might even be a poet! People always tell you to know your place in life. To play it safe and not to rock the boat. I never knew my place and I'm thankful for it."

"It's what I want. Just the *chance!*"

"I know son."

John Meredith reached into his pocket and took out two pound notes. He pressed them into Daniel's hand.

"I can't take this!"

"What time's your train tomorrow?"

"Nine. From Bangor."

"I'll come with you on the bus in the morning. You can borrow my quarry bag. And don't worry about your mother."

In the morning, before Gladys was up, they caught the bus to Bangor. At the station, Daniel bought his return ticket to Preston and shook his father's hand at the bottom of the steps which led up to Platform Two. Once up at the top he slung the quarry bag across his shoulder, turned round and waved to his father. John Meredith smiled and waved back. It was the last time Daniel ever saw him.

TWENTY

"Would Bethel Taid have liked me?"

Nain lowered her book and peered over the top of her glasses.

"What a strange question! Of course he would have liked you! You would have been his only grandson. He would have *loved* you."

"My other Taid gives me stuff. Pantglyn Taid. He even gave me his fishing rod."

"John was never one for fishing."

"What did he like doing?"

"Singing. That's how we met. I told you the story didn't I? I heard him singing in chapel. He had such a lovely voice."

"How did Bethel Taid die?"

Nain placed the book face down on her knees and took off her glasses.

"All these questions. Goodness me."

If my Mum had been there she would have slapped my thigh and told me to be quiet or say sorry for being so nosey but she'd gone to Caernarfon to do some shopping and my Dad was at work. It was only Nain and me.

"He came home one day from the quarry and sat down in that chair."

"*This* chair?"

Nain nodded.

"It was his favourite. He always said it fitted him perfectly – like the hand of an enormous giant. Dear me, he had such a vivid imagination sometimes. That evening he came in from work, sat down, took his big boots off over a sheet of newspaper like I always insisted – because they often got so muddy you see – and I went to get his supper ready. When I came back with the tray he was sitting back and his eyes were closed. I put the tray down carefully on the table over there and I shook him gently. 'John,' I said, 'you've got to eat your supper before it goes cold.' But he didn't move. I shook him even harder. And that's when I realised that he wasn't breathing. I knew he was dead."

"Was Dad there?"

"No," said Nain. "He wasn't."

TWENTY ONE

The smoke from the traffic was so thick Daniel felt as if he would have to slice it with a knife in order to breathe. Up until then the largest town he'd known had been Bangor but Preston must have been at least three or four times as big even after all the bombing. There were gaps in the streets like missing teeth in a punched mouth. Hitler must have thought there had been something worth destroying in Preston but heaven only knew what. People bumped into him from all directions and didn't even bother to apologise so Daniel stepped out of the way, back to the side of the pavement and leant against the station building wall. He clutched his father's tightly-packed quarry bag and watched everyone walk past him as if he wasn't there. He took out the card with the scribbled number on it which Tommy Kildare had given him the previous week and wondered if he should dial the number once again. He'd tried it on his arrival and a voice had told him to wait at the front of the station. But that had been over half an hour ago. Perhaps he should go back. His mother had been right. He didn't belong here.

"Daniel?"

He turned and saw a young man in a flat cap waving at him as he fought his way through the crowd.

"Shit," he said, when he finally arrived. "Sorry about being late. It's murder trying to get through these streets sometimes. That your bag? Let me take it. Let's get you out of this circus. I'm parked round the corner. Come on."

The stranger weaved like a pickpocket through the crowd,

dodging and ducking and somehow not managing to hit anyone – even whilst carrying the heavy quarry bag. The stranger turned a corner and led Daniel to a black four-door Austin Eight that was covered in dust. The car had clearly been parked in a hurry because it was lopsided, half on the pavement and half on the road. Most of the houses on the street were shells. There were no curtains behind the windows. No rooms either.

"Get in mate."

Daniel sank into the front seat.

"Ted Baines," said the young man, extending his hand. "Although everyone round here calls me Hoppy."

The Austin Eight's engine growled unhealthily as Hoppy bumped it off the pavement and along the shattered street.

"Why Hoppy?"

"Because of this," he said, tapping his left leg.

"What about it?"

"Not there is it?"

"I... don't understand."

"False," said Hoppy, tapping it harder this time so that Daniel now heard the distinct wooden knock. "Lost it down in Conduit Street after it was bombed. Part of a wall fell on it and crushed all the bones. Doctors said I had no chance of saving it so they took out a big saw and hacked it off. Shitty piece of luck really. I shouldn't have been down Conduit Street in the first place. I was only taking a short cut through to Soho Square to meet a bird."

"Isn't that in London?"

"Timbuctoo."

"Oh."

Clocking Daniel's serious and confused face Hoppy burst out laughing and nudged him.

"Of *course* London you idiot! Can't you tell from my accent?

I'm about as cockney as you can get. The Bow Bells were in my fucking lounge!" He shot his passenger a quick glance as he changed gear and slipped into a jokey plummy voice. "Unless of course my posh Eton education put you off the scent!"

Hoppy laughed again. This time Daniel joined in.

"So where you from then?" asked Hoppy.

"Wales."

"'Iekkyd da' and all that?"

"We do say that sometimes."

"You speak the lingo?"

"Yes."

"Say something."

"Maybe later."

"Fair enough. I feel pretty much the same when I'm asked to perform for the Royal Ballet. I can't do it to order I say, but I'll hop on down when the mood takes me."

The Austin Eight's engine coughed like an old donkey. The road was full of pot-holes and Hoppy did his best to avoid them.

"So what brought you up to Preston?" asked Daniel, feeling slightly more at ease in the Londoner's company.

"Same as you mate. The football. Before I lost this pin I was on the books up here. Not that I want to blow me own trumpet or anything but there had been quite a few of the big clubs that had wanted me. Everton were keen at one point. Bolton too. But I fancied Preston because of the king."

"The king?"

Hoppy shot him a glance.

"Tom Finney you berk."

Daniel laughed.

"Oh. Yes."

"Bit of a hero of mine," said Hoppy. "The Preston Plumber

they call him. Did you know that? Though some unkind hacks in the press have called the team 'The plumber and his ten drips'! You might meet him. He comes down to the ground quite a lot when he hasn't got a plumbing job on."

"Really?"

"I can introduce you."

"I wouldn't know what to say."

"Bollocks."

They stopped to allow a man and his dray horse to cross the road before Hoppy revved up the protesting engine once more and drove on along the cratered surface.

"Did it hurt?" asked Daniel, nodding down at the wooden leg.

"Yeah, at first. But then you get used to it. The only trouble is you think it's still there for a while. Put an end to my dreams of turning out for England at Wembley though. No bad thing I suppose. If you're going to lose your dreams, lose them while you're still young I say. I think my old man was a bit relieved to be honest. Not that he ever said anything. Anyway, I didn't want to go back south so I asked them if they had any odd jobs that needed doing up here and they kept me on. Now I make sure the kit's all in order, sort out the office stuff, fetch the balls for the training sessions." He glanced over at Daniel and winked mischievously. "And I also pick up the stars of the future like you from the station."

Hoppy swung left past a sign that read 'The Dale Training Grounds'. Ahead – half a mile or so along the bumpy gravel track – Daniel saw six football pitches lying side by side, all of them looking immaculately green and level – unlike the Oval's swampy slope. There was a small crowd of boys gathered at the end of the track and, next to them, Daniel saw a big man in a red tracksuit bouncing a football. Hoppy jolted the Austin Eight to a halt and got out.

"Sorry we're late Mr Mick," he said cheerfully. "But you know what they say don't you? Better late than never."

"Get changed," said Mr Mick, unsmilingly.

"Yes sir," said Daniel.

TWENTY TWO

The training pitch was less perfect than Daniel had thought. It was pock-marked with stud holes and skids – a chaotic cuneiform documenting the desperate efforts of hopefuls from all over the country to make it as professional footballers. The latest bunch of outfield contenders were in the centre circle being divided into teams by Mr Mick who was barking out names like a wolfhound, crossing them off the list on his notebook, telling them about formations and warning them that any nasty fouls would be punished by an instant sending off. Then Mr Mick came over and spoke to Daniel.

"Your job's simple," he said. "Just stop these bastards from scoring. See those blokes over there?" Mr Mick nodded towards four men in tracksuits who had suddenly appeared on the touch-line, all of them holding notebooks. "They're the ones you've got to impress today, not me. Forget me. And forget the other goal-keeper too. He's one of our young apprentices here to make up the numbers."

Mr Mick ran back to the centre circle.

"Remember lads, I'm the ref so keep your heads. No dirty business. Understood?"

There was an untidy chorus of affirmation and Mr Mick fumbled for the whistle around his neck.

"Let's get going then!"

He blew the whistle but when the game kicked off it was all played out in almost complete silence except for the shouts of the eager trialists and the thump of boot against ball. Daniel hadn't played in such a quiet match before. Usually there were taunts and insults from the supporters behind his goal depending on which end he was. He glanced furtively at the men on the touchline – at the strangers who were the masters of his fate. They were taking notes and occasionally pointing out certain moves or players but all their attention was focussed on the other side of the pitch. Daniel knew that over fifteen minutes had passed without him touching the ball. There hadn't even been a back-pass. He reckoned that if he'd sat cross-legged by the side of the goal reading a newspaper or writing a poem then it wouldn't have made the slightest bit of difference to the score. It was still 0-0.

And then, suddenly, it wasn't.

The young striker broke free and charged towards Daniel's penalty box. Instinctively Daniel came forward and tried to narrow the angle but he slipped in the mud and the striker saw his chance. The ball was a brown blur flashing past Daniel's right side and, without the sounds of a crowd, the rasp of leather against netting was painfully loud. Daniel was forced to suffer the indignity of having to retrieve the ball from the back of his own net.

"What the hell was that?"

It was half-time and, in the dressing room, Mr Mick was spraying Daniel with spittle.

"I slipped. I'm sorry."

"Fuck's sake son."

All the other hopefuls in the dressing room were clearly relieved not to be the targets of such a tirade themselves but the young apprentice goalkeeper tried to silently convey his sympathy because goalies were like that. They were different. Brothers in the firing line. Vulnerable as tail-gunners.

Mr Mick lowered his voice, placed an arm on Daniel's shoulder and dragged him to the far corner of the changing room. "We all get bad halves son. I've seen it loads of times. You kids get scared and I can't blame you. But let me tell you something. I was at fucking Dunkirk. Five days and five nights of Stukas swooping down and spraying the beach with bombs. Five days of you tensing your arse because you're scared you're either going to die, shit your pants or both! Now *that's* worth getting scared for. This is only football. You get me?"

Daniel nodded.

"You've got castles in Wales haven't you son?"

"Yes."

"Well be a fucking castle. For the next forty-five minutes you're made of stone. Now fuck off out of my sight."

During the second half Daniel tipped a shot over the bar, held on to three shots on target, found the winger with a perfectly judged throw, yelled at his defence and clapped his hands in encouragement. However, in the final minute of the game he let in another goal from the same brilliant young striker and he was 2-0 down. When Mr Mick blew the final whistle Daniel picked up his cap from the back of the goal and was mentally on the train back to Bangor, his dream well and truly over.

Hoppy was the first to greet him as he walked off the pitch.

"You were brilliant!"

"I let two in."

Daniel brushed past the Londoner towards the changing rooms but Hoppy followed and finally blocked his path.

"That tip over the bar was incredible!"

"Yeah, well."

Hoppy nodded in the direction of the men who had been watching and assessing from the touchline.

"Stanhope was impressed."

"Who's Stanhope?"

"The head coach."

Daniel sniffed dismissively and tried to edge past but Hoppy blocked him again.

"No really. I mean it. I heard him. I reckon they're going to ask you to hang on for another few days."

"Why are you being so kind?"

"Because I'm a kind fucker. Ain't you noticed?"

Daniel smiled. Then Mr Mick appeared and tapped him on the shoulder.

"Phone call for you son."

"For me?"

Mr Mick nodded. There was a serious look on his face. Too serious for football.

"It's your mother. She sounds upset."

TWENTY THREE

"Nice flowers Mr Meredith. Got a girlfriend?"

"Bugger off!"

The closer he got to Llys Meifor the more senseless the whole thing seemed and the faster John Meredith's heart began to beat. What if his father was right and that he was having ideas above his station? What if his future really was with Delyth?

He recognised the two boys who were taunting him. Waldo and Siôn. The sons of Pritchard and Trefor from the quarry.

"Is she a looker Mr Meredith?"

"*Bugger off!*"

He was wearing his best suit. The one he wore to chapel. Mr Warnham at the dry cleaners in Caernarfon had made sure it looked its best in plenty of time for tonight but had the old fool shrunk it in the process? Normally loose and comfortable the jacket was tight around his chest whilst the collar of his shirt felt as if it was slowly garroting him. Had he been given someone else's suit and shirt by mistake? They did say that old Warnham was going blind and becoming more careless.

"Those flowers for *her*, Mister Meredith?"

When he'd been sure his mother hadn't been watching he had plucked the best blooms from her prized patch in the back garden and rolled them up into a makeshift bouquet. She would be furious and there would be a scene but it was preferable to the embarrassment of going to the village shop and buying some. He knew how fast gossip travelled in the village. When a young man like John Meredith bought flowers it could only mean one thing. He was courting. Soon it would be the subject of gossip all over Bethel and everyone would know. And he didn't want anyone to know because it was likely to come to nothing anyway and people would laugh at him. John Meredith and one of the Morgan girls! How *outrageous*. The very *thought*.

He tried once again to remind himself that it was only an invitation to supper. It didn't mean they were actually seeing each other. And his mother would forgive him about the flowers in the end. That was what mothers always did.

"Are you *ill* Mister Meredith? Dr Morgan lives there."

He was standing by the wrought iron gates of Llys Meifor. He'd been there before of course, but only as a patient. That time he'd used the side entrance to the surgery on the west wing just like everyone else but now he was about to walk up the path which led to the front door. Tucking the flowers carefully under his arm, John Meredith reached into his pocket and took out a few coppers. He tossed them in the direction of Waldo and Siôn.

"Go and buy an ice cream."

"*Thank* you Mister Meredith!"

Delighted with their booty they kicked off on their bikes and tried to make it to the village shop before it closed.

John Meredith adjusted his tie, spruced up the bouquet a little and ventured down the crunchy path. It felt as long as a mile. The doorbell was the size of a saucer and there was a small white button in the middle with the word 'push' printed on it. His finger hovered. Once pressed there would be no turning back. He thought of Delyth and the life that was expected of him – coming home from the quarry in a few years to a lovely bowl of hot stew, two or three children, Delyth turning around from the stove, wiping her hands on her apron and kissing him on this cheek.

He shuddered. Pressed the bell.

TWENTY FOUR

When John Meredith stepped into the cavernous hallway of Llys Meifor for the first time he was immediately struck by the peculiar smell – a mixture of the medicinal and teak. The ornate handrail and bannisters on the staircase had been varnished and polished so meticulously he wondered how anyone could dare to touch it. A big grandfather clock in the corner lazily ticked off the seconds as if they didn't really matter and, directly above the telephone – the only private telephone John Meredith had ever seen – there was a painting of some sheep grazing on a mountainside.

"Abraham Lewis," said Dr Morgan, referring to the painting. "A member of the Welsh Pastoral School. Are you an admirer of the arts Mr Meredith?"

"Not really. But it's very nice."

Dr Morgan winced.

"You'd better come through."

John Meredith had thought that seeing Gladys might come as something of a relief but, when he entered the dining room and saw her standing next to her sister by the fireside he felt more terrified than ever. She looked so elegant and lovely and the flowers in his hand suddenly felt like sticks.

"Oh, how lovely," said Mrs Morgan, stepping forward to take them and tinkling a little handbell. "I'll get Beti to put some in a vase."

John knew that Mrs Morgan was renowned around the village for putting on airs and graces but she appeared to be even more determined to put on a show that evening. Was it for his benefit? Over by the fireside Kate nudged her sister. Gladys smiled and tried to hide it. They were like schoolgirls.

"Well don't just stand there like a statue," said Kate, coming forward, "what will you have? A whiskey? Or a brandy perhaps?"

He followed Kate up to the drinks cabinet. He had never seen so many bottles in one house. And all of them were so shiny and clean. Now that the flowers had been taken away from him he didn't know what to do with his hands.

"I'm... not sure."

"Whiskey's good," said Gladys, still standing over by the fireplace. "We're allowed it sometimes. As long as it's got plenty of water in it."

"I'll have some of that then," said John Meredith, adding briskly, "although I'm not much of a drinking man."

As Kate handed him the glass she leant across and whispered.

"It's alright. God's not watching you Mr Meredith. We gave him the night off."

He wasn't sure how to take Kate sometimes. Was she laughing at him or did she just find life in general rather comical? She clinked his glass.

"Bottoms up," she said.

John Meredith took a mouthful of whiskey. He didn't like the taste. He'd never liked whiskey but he didn't want to appear unsophisticated. He felt like a pauper at a palace. Llys Meifor wasn't a palace exactly. Although it did contain a princess.

"We were thinking you might give us a song later on Mr Meredith," said Kate, with a teasing smile.

"*John*, please."

"Oh yes of course," said Mrs Morgan from the other side of

the room. "You must sing for us. I'd forgotten about your lovely voice."

"It's really nothing special Mrs Morgan."

"Nonsense," said Dr Morgan, "we've heard you in chapel. A very pleasing baritone if I may say so. Everyone in Bethel agrees. I daresay you could easily compete at the National Eisteddfod if you put your mind to it."

"We'll get you round the piano later," said Kate, still smiling. "Gladys can play and you can sing. What could be more perfect?"

John Meredith wanted to run out of the room. It had been a big mistake. His father had been right. He didn't belong in Llys Meifor's world. He just worked at the quarry. He wasn't a doctor or a university student. He didn't like whisky. He was dreading the meal because he didn't know which knife and fork to use. The last thing he felt like doing was singing.

TWENTY FIVE

"You can open your eyes now."

Gladys had been told to close them for five minutes but it had felt more like ten. She had listened as John Meredith scratched something into the wood. Once, her curiosity getting the better of her, she had tried to peep but he'd spotted it and told her, mock-sternly, to keep her eyes firmly shut. Smiling, she had obeyed. Now that he'd finished and told her it was okay to look she finally saw the result of John Meredith's fervent industry. He had carved both their names into the back of the bench with his pen-knife, surrounded by a heart.

"My father will have a *fit!*"

"Then you mustn't tell him."

Gladys was still open-mouthed in shock. But secretly she felt delighted. She laughed and sat back.

"What a peculiar thing to do!"

John Meredith folded the blade of his pen-knife and slid it back into his pocket. The goldfish pond plopped gently every few seconds. After dinner, Kate had been appointed as their chaperone and now she was pretending to be interested in a potential frog on the other side of the pond at a discreet distance.

"I got you out of singing," said Gladys nervously.

"Yes," said John Meredith. "Thank you. That would have been terrible. I would have been out of tune and forgotten all the words."

"I'm so sorry you had to go through all that."

"At least now I know which knife and fork to use. It might be useful at the quarry come lunchtime."

Gladys giggled but it petered out after a few seconds. They listened to the breeze whispering through the bushes and to the invisible fish rippling the pond.

"Thank you for the flowers."

"I stole them."

Gladys feigned shock, but then she smiled.

"Who from?"

"Our back garden, so maybe it doesn't count."

"Stealing is stealing, John Meredith!"

"I suppose. Although your sister tells me God's got the night off."

"Oh, God never has the night off," said Gladys. "You should know that."

About three weeks before John Meredith finally plucked up the courage to propose, Gladys Morgan let it slip during one of their chaperoned evening strolls around Bethel that she'd run out of jars and pots for her homemade marmalade. John Meredith said he'd have a look around his mother's kitchen to see what he could find. The following day he came to Llys Meifor with five perfectly scoured jam pots – complete with lids – together with three or four tins which he said might come in useful. When Gladys saw that one of them had been a tin of rat poison she almost hurled it away in horror but John assured her that it had been thoroughly cleaned out. Seeing how worried she was he offered to take it back and throw it in the bin but Kate thought it was hilarious. She suggested it would be a great place to keep the sugar. Maybe, she said, with joy in her eyes, one day it would be a fantastic practical joke to play on their parents. So Gladys relented. She took the jar, filled it with sugar, popped on the lid and hid it behind some of the other tins and jars in the pantry where it lay forgotten for many, many years.

TWENTY SIX

Only The Hangman knew what was really going on. He knew their tricks and he understood their methods. The objective and endgame, as ever, was the complete and utter colonization of Wales and someone had to stand up in the name of resistance. The time for words was over. Other methods were now needed. The ridiculous pantomime that was the Investiture of Prince Charles in Caernarfon Castle was less than a week away and after that he would be known as the Prince of Wales. *The Prince of Fucking Wales*! And the stupid people of Bethel – just like all the other stupid people across the length and breadth of the land – had swallowed the propaganda like willing idiots, waving their little Union Jacks at every opportunity, hanging them up in their front windows, singing 'God Save the Queen' on buses and buying dumb trinkets, instruments of oppression in the form of souvenir tea-towels and mugs. The shops of Caernarfon were festooned in red, white and blue and there wasn't a single red dragon to be seen – the red dragon which signified and represented the true Prince of Wales, the one who had been slain and dismembered by the cowardly English at Cilmeri in 1282. Wales was sleepwalking into disaster and political oblivion. The Hangman was one of the few true soldiers left.

They were outside his house, on the other side of the road in a surf green Volkswagen. Two MI5 men. One sipping tea from a plastic cup. The other holding a brick-sized walkie talkie. The *Daily Post* flopped through the front door and The Hangman stepped back from the window. In the kitchen, Leah heard the metallic slap of the letter box too and rolled her eyes. She allowed her hands to sink into the hot suds and waited for the explosion.

"I *knew* it! I just *bloody well knew it!*"

The Hangman stormed into the kitchen and showed her the letters page.

"Didn't they publish it?" she offered.

"Of *course* not!" He slapped the *Daily Post* as if it was a disobedient dog. "What can you expect from a royalist rag like this?"

"We can change papers if you like? Get the *Express* or something?"

The Hangman ignored her.

"It's supposed to be a paper for Wales," he said. "But, of course it's printed in Liverpool. Says it all really doesn't it? They've given up using armies, now they use newspapers! To create slaves you first take away their language, then you take away their fucking history!"

"Watch your language! Llew is upstairs!"

"I don't care! It's about time he learned something about his own heritage. All he gets at school is imperialist propaganda. And now this bloody rag has been neutered by the establishment! It's a fucking conspiracy!"

Leah dried her hands on the tea-towel. Trying to console her husband because the paper hadn't published one of his protest poems had recently become something of a daily occurrence. When the fuss was all over and when Caernarfon Castle was back to normal then perhaps things wouldn't be so tense. She laid a hand gently on his shoulder.

"Why don't you write another one?"

But The Hangman shook her off.

"What's the point?"

The Hangman punched the *Daily Post* so hard that the pages separated and fanned out all across the kitchen floor. Then he leant against the fridge and popped an Embassy in his mouth. He lit it, inhaled, inspected the tip for no apparent reason and inhaled again.

"Are they still out there?" asked Leah.

"Same two as yesterday," said The Hangman, blowing smoke up at the ceiling. "Same car too. A green Beetle."

"Not the kind of car you expect from spies really is it?"

The Hangman grabbed his jacket.

"Where are you going?"

"*Out!*"

TWENTY SEVEN

There was an eskimo in the curtains and his name was Miko. He only came out on certain stormy nights when I was in bed and when the big damson tree next door hurled terrifying shadows across the window like splashes of black paint. Miko told me not to worry. It couldn't hurt me. We spoke in English, not Welsh. There was no way an eskimo could understand Welsh but I figured that even someone who had spent all his life in the snow-swept tundra of the North Pole hunting seals and whipping husky teams into fierce blizzards could understand basic English. I could go for weeks without hearing from him. As a full-time eskimo he was probably busy and couldn't afford to drop his fishing pole or his husky team just because his friend in Wales was scared of a stupid damson tree. But Miko made it when he could. And he always told me not to worry. I whispered things back to him and he just told me he would sort it and that everything would be okay. And they always were. During the day it was difficult to imagine that there was an eskimo in the curtains because daylight always made things look really normal. The frightening damson tree looked so harmless in the morning and I could never understand why the thin wiry branches had scared me so much. I sometimes felt slightly stupid about needing to call upon an eskimo friend who lived in the curtains and I never told anyone about it.

After Nain had died we had moved into a new house down the same street and my Dad had named it Man Heulog. It meant 'sunny spot' but the sun hardly ever shone over Bethel. Not even in summer. The best thing about the new house was that it was modern – built with bricks not old stone like Nain's house – and it had a huge back garden. It was rectangular, flat and completely green. From my bedroom window I sometimes tried to pretend that I was looking down on Wembley. I'd never been to Wembley but I'd seen it on television and now the garden looked even more like a proper pitch because my Dad had built a goal at the far end and painted it white. I'd said that I'd wanted to be a goalkeeper and he had offered to train me so, when the weather wasn't too bad, he would get the ball from the garage and we'd go out for a session while my Mum sometimes watched from the kitchen window for a bit. My Dad would launch shot after shot at me and the ball slapped painfully against my legs.

"Don't hit them so hard!" I protested.

My Dad thought it was funny.

"Is that how you think football is?" he said. "Do you think goalkeepers say to George Best or Bobby Charlton if they wouldn't mind not hitting the ball too hard because it hurts their legs?"

He took pity on me sometimes because he knew that my Mum was watching from the kitchen window and he slipped in an easy one just to make me feel better but he was far too competitive to make a habit of it. When he kept scoring I would sulk sometimes and kick the post or stamp my feet but he would tell me off and say that proper footballers didn't do that. I knew he was wrong because I'd seen them do it on *Match of the Day* but I never argued with him. In his purple tracksuit he was scary. Like an enemy.

When it was my turn to shoot at goal I hardly ever got one past him. Even though he was too old by now to be a proper goalie he could dive around like a kid and his hands and feet were always faster than the ball however hard I kicked it. He didn't care how muddy or dirty he got – his whole body became a wall and its sole mission in life was to stop that ball from going past. He never took his eyes off the ball. I would try to dodge and feint but it was no good. Even my best shots thumped harmlessly into his chest or into his hands.

I was never going to be a footballer. It was sad to think that I was never going to be on *Match of the Day* being interviewed by David Coleman after scoring the winning goal at Wembley but at least there were other things I could think about doing. Like being a dinosaur expert. I could name almost every dinosaur from any period – from the Triassic to the Cretaceous – just by looking at a picture and not even my Dad could do that. My Mum said she was going to buy me an electric guitar for Christmas so I could learn to play and be a pop star on *Top of the Pops*. There were plenty of other things besides football in my world. Some of them were secret. Like the gun. Not even Miko knew about the gun.

TWENTY EIGHT

Every Tuesday evening Cerwyn Evans went down to the Wilson Club in Caernarfon to sit round the table in the corner where T.J. Watcyn, the great Bard, held his informal poetry classes. The four young men were regulars – himself, Trefor Rowland, John Tŷ Mawr and Rhydian Vaughan. Each week they turned up with a clutch of their own poems to await T.J. Watcyn's merciless judgement. Most would be dismissed with a curt laugh of contempt and a swift strike of the pen.

"No good," he would grunt, hurling back the typed sheets of poems in a sudden flurry. "Next!"

Cerwyn Evans offered up his two new poems, one about the majesty of Mount Orwig and the other about the swelling of the tides on the Menai. T.J. Watcyn held the sheets up to the light and squinted as if he was checking a counterfeit pound note. He mouthed the poem to himself, feeling around for any latent musicality whilst also assessing the mathematical accuracy of the ancient cynghanedd alliterative system. Cerwyn looked nervously at the other young men around the table. John Tŷ Mawr raised his eyebrows in an expression of hope. Trefor Rowland and Rhydian Vaughan pursed their lips and nodded. So far so good. At least Cerwyn's poems had merited a second reading by T.J. Watcyn and hadn't been immediately thrown back in disgust.

"Not bad," he grunted eventually. "It doesn't ring and the cynghanedd is mechanical rather than musical but not bad."

"Thank you Mr Watcyn."

Praise, however faint, was somehow more difficult to deal with that the customary contempt. Cerwyn glanced nervously at his companions and, although they nodded in approval, he knew that they were seething. Cerwyn was the most promising poet among their number. The improvement in his work since T.J. Watcyn had begun his informal gathering at the Wilson Club six months earlier had been the most dramatic, but, even so, there were times when Cerwyn wondered whether friendship was more important to him than poetry. Not that it was of course. Nothing was more important than poetry.

Refreshed by another double scotch which had been bought for him by his eager students, T.J. Watcyn lit up his pipe and expounded yet again on his favourite subject. The cynghanedd.

"You see boys," he said, "the English have their Wordsworths and Byrons and Shelleys – they even have the genius that was William Shakespeare. But for all their stars they don't have our music. The music of the words. Now, for some, I'm sure the cynghanedd must seem like an outdated alliterative system completely unsuited to the nuances and rhythms of modern, everyday speech and you know what boys? I would agree with them. Oh yes. There's no doubt about it that the cynghanedd, for all it's beauty, does not react well to current idioms. There is a stubbornness to it which rubs uncomfortably against the task of representing life in Wales here in the nineteen fifties."

He leant forward dramatically.

"But that's the whole fucking point! If I want a true picture of what life is like here in Caernarfon I can go out and take a photo-graph or buy the *Caernarfon and Denbigh Herald*! I'm talking about poetry! Music!"

Leaning back in his chair and puffing again at the pipe he opened his mouth to continue his diatribe when he was gently interrupted by a polite cough from the far side of the room.

"Can we help you?" said T.J. Watcyn, irritably.

The four disciples looked round and saw a dark-haired youth, probably five or six years younger than all of them. He was dressed smartly in a dark suit and his pitch-black hair, thick and straight, had been Brylcreemed so thoroughly that it appeared to shine like ebony. He was slim and athletic-looking. In his hand he held a folder. He cleared his throat like a schoolboy.

"I... understand that you teach poetry sir."

"*Teach poetry?*" repeated T.J. Watcyn. "You think poetry can be *taught*? You can teach a child to walk but it takes a poet to dance! Dancing is something you're born with! Do you dance?"

The young stranger shook his head.

"Is there music in your soul boy?"

"My... father was a good singer. Hymns mainly."

"Hymns eh?"

T.J. Watcyn studied him. Then he pointed towards a chair.

"Pull that up. Come and sit down boy."

The young stranger seemed uncertain. He straightened his tie, pulled on his cuffs and walked over, sitting down on the edge of the chair.

"So you're a poet?"

"I'm not sure sir."

"Show me."

The stranger slid out a poem from his folder and handed it to T.J. Watcyn. As he read the poem to himself, T.J. Watcyn's lips mouthed the words and Cerwyn and the others glanced at each other knowingly, waiting for the moment when the young newcomer's effort would be hurled back at him in disgust.

But that moment never came.

T.J. Watcyn went back to the top again and read the whole

thing a second time, but this time his free hand waved in the air as if he was conducting a piece of music only he could hear. He rested the poem on his lap and sat forward.

"What's your name?"

"Daniel, sir."

"I knew it," said John Tŷ Mawr, clapping his hands and turning to the others. "I knew I'd seen him somewhere before. It's Daniel Meredith. Weren't you in goal for the canaries?"

Daniel turned to him and nodded almost with embarrassment.

"I was."

"Didn't you once get a trial with Bolton?"

"Preston."

T.J. Watcyn made some kind of contemptuous rattling noise in the back of his throat which sounded more animal than human.

"Saturday," he said, addressing Daniel. "What are your plans?"

Daniel was confused.

"Nothing."

"Good. We start from Caernarfon Maes at ten. Bring warm clothes."

"Where are we going?"

"Up Mount Orwig," said the bard. "To the very peak!"

TWENTY NINE

The germs had burrowed into Llew's body and were now impossible to get rid of.

"What kind of germs are they?"

It was Hari who had summoned up the courage to pose the question we had all wanted to ask. Farming Boy swung casually on the thick rope like an ape born to the jungle, the branches creaking under his extra weight.

"Tiny black ones. You can't really see them. But if you did, under a microscope or something, they'd look like a woodlouse. Or a spider."

We all looked at each other, imagining such a horrific thing and scratching our arms because we were all suddenly itchy. Farming Boy kept swinging on the rope that someone, no-one knew exactly who, had tied to the thick tree trunk at the bottom of the field by the new council houses. We didn't know why he was called Farming Boy. Hari said it was because he'd once tried to steal a real tractor.

"The worst thing is that you can catch them."

"How?" asked Hari.

"If you touch Llew then the germs can just hop off him and land on you."

"But," I said, wary because everyone knew that Llew was my best friend. "I thought you said they'd burrowed under his skin."

Farming Boy skidded the swing to a halt. He gave me a look, the same look he'd given me just before he'd punched me in the stomach a week earlier outside the village shop for no reason at all except that he'd felt like it. He was like that. Unpredictable. He was like a bomb you couldn't hear tick.

"Know about germs do you?"

"No," I said.

"Well let me tell you. These germs eat you from the inside. First of all they eat the soft bits, all the flesh and guts and stuff and then they start on your brain. That's when you go mad. But most people kill themselves before that bit. I saw it on telly. Someone in Africa had it. Everyone in the village ran away from them and in the end they burned down their house."

"But how did Llew get the germs?" asked Hari. "He's never been to Africa."

"The germs are everywhere. They don't have to come from Africa. My uncle told me about them. He's a doctor in Liverpool."

Farming Boy's uncle had led the most incredible life. Over the years he'd been a soldier out in Vietnam, a spy, Mick Jagger's best mate, a racing car engineer, one of the men who had built the Severn Bridge, a film director, a trucker in America, a boxer who had gone ten rounds with Muhammad Ali and, now, a doctor. He kept saying that, one day, he was going to drive over to Bethel to see them all in his Rolls-Royce and bring Ringo Starr with him. But so far there had always been a last minute excuse.

"The germs are in the air," said Farming Boy. "That's what my uncle said. They're probably all around us now but we can't see them because they're so small. They only pick on certain people. They probably landed on Llew because his Mum is so pig ugly and because of what his Dad does to kittens."

"What does your Dad do to kittens?"

We were in Llew's back garden two days later eating a jam sandwich.

"He kills them."

"Doesn't he like them?"

"Dunno."

"Is that why they call him The Hangman?"

"He doesn't hang them."

The new council houses in Bethel didn't have great back gardens. They were small and bumpy and, in Llew's, the grass was thin and coarse, only becoming thick in the corners. Tucked in at the end of the garden was The Hangman's old shed. Planks of wood hung off it like something from an old cowboy town on telly and the one tiny window was curtained by cobwebs. I'd never been inside. Once, when the door had been left open, I'd peeked in and seen a table and a big barrel. There were also piles and piles of old newspapers lying on top of each other and the whole place was buzzing with bluebottles.

"He's going to do some tonight after tea," said Llew. "Come over if you like."

At first I hadn't been too sure if I wanted to see The Hangman kill some kittens but Llew seemed so casual about it and there was a part of me that was quite curious.

"Scared?"

"No," I said.

But I was lying. I was feeling a bit weird. I'd been invited round for tea and now the baked beans with pork sausages that Llew's Mum had plopped out of a tin and served up on soldiers was as heavy as a regiment on my stomach and I wondered if the sight of kittens being killed would make me throw up. Out in the back garden The Hangman paced up and down smoking a fag and checking his watch. The door to his shed was open and the lid from the big wooden barrel had been pushed back. Llew nudged me.

"It's full of water," he whispered.

Llew's Mum came in to the kitchen wiping her hands on a tea-towel and saw us both in the doorway looking out at the shed.

"Haven't you two boys got anything better to do?"

"He's about to do some more kittens Mum."

"Oh, for God's sake. I wish he'd stop."

She rolled her eyes, replaced the tea-towel on a rack and went back into the lounge where the TV news was on quietly.

Out in the back garden The Hangman began whistling. I recognised the song. It was *Oh Happy Day* by the Edwin Hawkins Singers. I'd seen it on *Top of the Pops*. Then the man with the kittens arrived. It was Mr Lewis from chapel. He'd always ruffled my hair and poked me affectionately in the chest after the morning services. This time though, instead of being smartly dressed in his dark chapel suit and with his grey hair carefully oiled back, he was wearing a shabby brown overcoat and a wide-brimmed hat. When he saw me standing in the doorway he pulled his hat down over his face and turned his body sideways as if this would make him less recogniseable. He was holding a heavy-looking linen bag which was moving and squeaking. He handed it to The Hangman together with what looked like a five pound note. Then, without looking back, Mr Lewis pulled down his hat even lower over his face and walked off as quickly as he could.

The Hangman stubbed out his cigarette and took the writhing linen bag into the shed. He tied it shut, pushed back the lid of the barrel, dropped the bag in the water and held it down for over three minutes. I held my breath, imagining I was one of the poor kittens trapped inside the linen bag but when I felt my face going red I had to stop.

The Hangman took out the dripping bag. It was now still and silent. He shook off some of the water and rammed it down into the bin. Wiping his hands on his trousers he closed the shed door and walked up towards the kitchen. Throughout it all he never stopped whistling.

THIRTY

"When I was born I was so ugly the midwife went into shock and ran screaming from the house. The doctor took one look at my shrivelled up face, declared it to be that of the devil himself, backed away, tripped over the chamber pot and hit his head against the wall. You can imagine, the news spread quickly that a diabolical baby had been born and soon there was a large crowd outside the house, curious to see if I was as ugly as everyone said. *'Show us the baby'*, they all shouted. Like something from a football match. *'Show us the baby! Show us the baby! Show us the baby!'* So my mother lifted me up for all to see. She moved the blanket away from my face and everyone fainted from shock."

"Don't be silly," said Miriam.

"It's true," said Leah. "I was the ugliest baby ever born."

They were on their lunch break and Caernarfon was dead. They'd only served three customers that day and the rain was unlikely to make things better in the afternoon.

"You're not ugly."

"Too slow! But it's okay. I've got used to it. You don't have to be nice just because you're my friend."

Leah smiled.

"I always knew I was ugly. Did you always know you were pretty?"

"I'm not pretty!"

"You are and you know it! I've seen the way boys look at you in The Britannia."

Miriam lifted the coffee to her lips and blew away the froth to reveal a light brown oval.

"I don't care about other boys."

Leah sipped her coffee too. But she kept her eyes on her friend.

"Has he written this week?"

"Twice."

"And you're really going to do it? Turn Catholic I mean?"

Miriam put down the coffee cup.

"Pádraig says he's going to talk to the priest. He tells me that all I have to do is a bit of studying, go to some Bible classes, promise to be a good Catholic girl and that's it! We can get married!"

"What about your parents though?"

"They'll get used to it."

Leah nodded. She sipped her coffee. Miriam felt a bit guilty discussing her own imminent happiness so she leant in and placed her hand on Leah's.

"You'll find someone," she said. "Someone special."

Leah raised her eyebrows cynically.

"Tell you what," said Miriam. "This Saturday we'll go out and we'll have a laugh. Just you and me. We'll dress up, go out to The Britannia and have some drinks and a gossip. How's that?"

Leah broke into a smile.

"Sounds like fun."

"Good. Now come on. We'd better shift. We're already five minutes late. It's pissing down. But you can share my brolly."

Miriam was sure there had been nothing in the Ten Commandments that forbade lying, especially a white lie that did no one any harm. Despite this, and just to be on the safe side, she did sometimes ask God for his forgiveness before she went to bed at night. She hoped he would understand because, after all, he was supposed to embody Love. And what was Friendship if not another manifestation of Love? She really wished Leah wasn't the ugliest girl she had ever seen but all the wishing in the world couldn't change her face. In the months they had worked together at Mr Oliver's shoe shop she had eventually got used to the two big warts on Leah's chin, the slightly bulging eyes, the protruding front teeth and the thin hair which looked like it belonged to a woman three times her age. But Leah had inner beauty. She was kind and loyal. If ever Miriam was late because of the bus, or if they were ever caught giggling in the store cupboard, Leah would take the blame and she would suffer the full force of Mr Oliver's wrath. If only she could find a boyfriend. Someone who could be nice to her and love her. Miriam knew how wonderful it was to be swept off her feet and she wanted that for her friend too. As a child, her mother had always told her that there was someone for everyone in this world. Now though, Miriam reflected that she was probably wishing it hadn't been someone who would take her all the way across the sea to Ireland.

THIRTY ONE

When she stepped off the Whiteways bus from Pantglyn that Saturday night Miriam wondered if the rain was actually strong enough to punch holes in her umbrella. Raindrops the size of locusts splashed the puddles and, with so much water in Caernarfon's Maes, it looked as if the buses were boats. The nearest pub to the buses was The Castle Arms but it was the one where all the rough boys went and where fights always broke out. Even though it was still quite early she could see that some of the lads in The Castle Arms were already drunk and were shouting out through the windows and encouraging all the girls to go in. They leant out of the windows, fags in the corners of their mouths, not even caring if they got wet or spilled their pints and each time a new girl went in the louts issued loud and boorish cheers.

Leah stepped out of the purple bus from Penygroes and ran over to her friend. The rain was drumming so hard on her umbrella that Miriam almost had to resort to lip-reading.

"I thought it might stop," shouted Leah. "But I think it's actually getting worse!"

"I like your dress!"

"What?"

"Your dress! Such a lovely bright red! Is it new?"

"It's no good! This rain!"

"Shall we make a run for it?"

"Okay. But not too fast. I can never catch up with you!"

"I'll give you a head start!"

"Okay! Wish me luck!"

Leah hobbled gracelessly through the puddles and Miriam could see that her new red dress was getting soaked. Some of the drunk boys from The Castle Arms saw her and began to cheer her on although Miriam noticed that Leah wasn't being encouraged to go in and join them. After a few seconds Miriam followed her friend towards The Britannia – the puddles slashing coldly across her ankles and the wind wrestling for her brolly. She laughed as she overtook Leah.

"Come on," she said, "We're almost there!"

The Britannia was a little more sedate and there were no louts cheering them on from the windows but, when she looked up, Miriam did see one man standing in the doorway with a pint of beer in his hand. He seemed to be staring directly at her. She found it a bit unnerving but, after a few seconds he was gone.

Leah caught up, breathless and soaking wet.

"You go in first," said Miriam. "I'll let you win for once!"

THIRTY TWO

The Britannia was busy and there was raucous singing coming from the far corner. Miriam didn't recognise the song but it sounded Irish, like one of the ones Pádraig used to sing to himself when he was fixing a plug or making straw bobbies. What would he say if he found out she was out on a Saturday night in the Britannia? He wouldn't like it. Even though she was with Leah he would still have been annoyed.

"Gin and tonic?" asked Leah.

"Why not?"

"Mind my bag."

As she watched Leah walk towards the bar Miriam felt sorry for her. The rain had flattened her curls and the thick powder that she'd dabbed on to try to hide the warts on her chin had been washed away.

Miriam took some lipstick out of her handbag and applied it carefully using her compact mirror. It kept steaming up so she had to constantly wipe it on her sleeve. Eventually she gave up and popped both lipstick and compact back into her handbag. She ruffled up her soaking locks as best she could and watched the droplets land on the table in chaotic rows.

How long had it been since she had last been here with Pádraig? Weeks. Months. It all seemed so long ago. Almost like a different time. When she looked around The Britannia she saw smiling girls with smiling boys and everyone having a good time. She wished Pádraig was there now. He would have raised his pint of Guinness and gone across to the piano demanding some more Irish ballads from the singers and, when he sang – unlike the locals – he would have been in tune and he would have known all the words!

She glanced across idly to the other side of the bar and her eyes rested upon a group of young men who were laughing and pointing at one of their number. Miriam recognised him immediately as the man she'd seen standing in the window as she'd been running through the rain. It wasn't clear what was going on but he had obviously done or said something that had amused his friends even though he himself didn't look at all happy. Then her heart skipped because one of the young men teasing him was Daniel. He looked up, caught her eye and looked slightly embarrassed as he waved half-heartedly to her but Miriam's heart snapped like elastic and she didn't wave back. She was relieved when Leah came back with the drinks. Placing the two gins on the table Leah sat down and clocked Daniel too.

"Isn't he the one you went to the Wilson Club with the other week?"

"Don't stare at them!"

"I'm not staring. Hey, one of them's coming over."

"Oh God!"

"Not your poet. Relax! It's one of the others. Here, have one of these and try to look as if you don't care."

"But I *don't* care!"

Miriam took the cigarette Leah had offered. Leah lit it. When Miriam sat back she saw that the man who had been staring at her from the doorway was now standing next to their table and that he was clearly nervous. In her eyes he wasn't a bad looking fellow although he did have the look of a man who'd had one pint too many. His hair had fallen down over his face slightly and the top two buttons of his shirt were open. She could see that his tie had been coiled up into his pocket.

Miriam had been prepared to deliver the well-practised lie that she was waiting for her boyfriend and that he would be arriving any second but, as it turned out, the staring man didn't seem interested in her at all. He was looking at Leah.

"Can I buy you a drink?" he asked her.

"Just got one thanks."

"Crisps then."

"I don't want crisps."

"At least tell me your name."

"Leah."

"Cerwyn."

He extended his hand. Then, realizing it was wet with beer he wiped it on his trousers hurriedly and offered it again but Leah simply stared at it. Then at him.

"Well, it was nice to meet you Cerwyn. Thanks for the offer of the crisps. Now, if you'll excuse me, I'm out with my friend tonight and we have many important things to discuss."

He ignored her. He grabbed a stray stool and plonked himself down beside her.

"Marry me."

"*What?*"

"I'm serious."

"Why would I want to marry you? I've never even seen you before!"

"Are you engaged?"

"No."

"Got a boyfriend?"

"No."

"Marry me then."

"You're mad! I've never heard anything so ridiculous in my life!"

Three months later they were married in Caernarfon's Salem chapel and Miriam was the chief bridesmaid.

THIRTY THREE

With every passing year it seemed as if the crown or the chair at the National Eisteddfod was getting further away from his grasp. For five years in a row he'd stuffed his neatly typed odes into a brown envelope, making sure nothing got creased or bent, licked the seal and sent them off by first class post. Why hadn't he won? Was there a conspiracy against him? In theory that shouldn't be possible since none of the adjudicators in the major literary competitions of the crown and chair at the National Eisteddfod ever received the entrants' real names until the winner had been decided – all they had were pseudonyms so that nepotism and personal prejudice were both eliminated from the process. Records of the entrants' real names were kept in the Eisteddfod office under lock and key. The winners of both competitions were only informed by letter by the end of April at the latest and sworn to secrecy until the ceremony in August.

If it wasn't the National Eisteddfod pitting themselves against him then perhaps it was the English establishment? That made more sense because the way The Hangman saw it there was nothing wrong with his poetry. His cynghanedd was sound. Water-tight. So it must have been the politics. The forces of English imperialism had penetrated the inner sanctuary of the most prestigious Welsh language cultural event and deemed that poems which took political and cultural colonization as their central theme were too hot to handle in the year of the Investiture of Prince Charles.

He blamed the spineless Welsh traitors who'd allowed all this to happen; the arse-lickers like Secretary of State for Wales George Thomas, the donkey-like Welsh public waving their pathetic Union Jack flags, the gutless Welsh press with their sycophantic puff stories, the kowtowing Mayor of Caernarfon and his ridiculous wife both wetting themselves with pleasure as they anticipated shaking hands with Prince Charles, the Queen, Prince Phillip and that oily warmonger Lord Mountbatten. He blamed the fag-smoking tart Princess Margaret. He blamed Harold Wilson and his weathervane socialism. He blamed all of these people. But most of all, The Hangman blamed Daniel.

"Are you following me?"

The Hangman had stopped and had turned around to face the two men. They were smaller than he'd expected. But then he'd only seen them sitting in the green Volkswagen outside his house. Now, standing in their suits and shades halfway along the path through the field which led towards the village shop, they looked out of place, almost exotic.

"We don't want any trouble, Mr Evans."

"Who mentioned trouble?"

The two men looked at each other. The first one took a packet of Rothmans out of his suit pocket, shook out a cigarette, lit it, and flicked the match expertly into the long grass.

"These are sensitive times Mr Evans," he said, revealing a heavy London accent. "The eyes of the world are going to be on this place in a few days time. The Investiture of your new Prince of Wales."

"He's not *my* bloody prince. Now leave me alone."

He turned to walk away but the two men jumped ahead of him and blocked his path. The Londoner reached into the inside pocket of his suit and took out an envelope. Inside were what appeared to be a sheaf of newspaper cuttings held together with a clip. The Londoner read one out loud.

" *'The only way that Wales will ever be truly free is through violent struggle. Everything else has been attempted and everything has so far failed. The repressive English establishment cannot be trusted to respect and protect our culture, heritage and language because their sole objective is to destroy it. Just like their imperialist lust crushed the indigenous cultures of a third of the world under their barbarous empire!'* "

The Londoner looked at The Hangman briefly for a reaction but there wasn't one so he started reading out the second clip.

" *'We should take our cue from the Irish, our Celtic brethren, and take up arms. The IRA are represented as terrorists by the politicians and the despicable media but we know that, in reality, they are freedom fighters in a battle to the death with the very forces that are out to try to crush them. If the British government will not listen to our words perhaps they will listen to the cries of their dying children.'* "

The Londoner looked up.

"I didn't write that," said The Hangman. Then he reddened slightly. "Not the last one."

"We know," said the Londoner. "The second clip was written by a guy calling himself Cadno. Not his real name obviously. Cadno's real name, as you probably know, is Llyr Price and he is – surprise surprise – a member of that group of boy soldiers the Free Wales Army. An organization which I believe you have great sympathy for?"

"Piss off," said The Hangman

He tried to move on again but the Londoner grabbed his shoulders.

"You know him I think. This Cadno guy."

"I can't choose my friends now, is that it?"

"So he is a friend?"

The Hangman paused. He opened his mouth to say something but thought better of it. There was a sense of a situation brewing which could easily get out of control if he wasn't careful. If these guys really were from the security services then they could make his life difficult if he did or said anything reckless.

"I can't say he's a friend exactly."

The Londoner smiled, released his grip and stubbed out his half-smoked cigarette.

"But you sympathise?"

"Am I allowed to sympathise? You tell me. If not I'll just go along with the orthodoxy, I'll cheer the new prince and wave a plastic Union Jack. Is that what I should do?"

"There's a list."

"What are you talking about?"

"Known agitators," said the Londoner. "Do you know where Llyr Price is now?"

"No."

"We do. Have a guess."

"Siberia?"

"Brighton."

"What?"

"Nice little break for all the family. A couple of weeks away by the sea, far away from all the everyday woes of his life as a teacher. And, of course, far away from the Investiture. When it's all over we'll bring him back. Who knows, he may bring us a stick of rock."

"Oh I get it! You're threatening to send me and my family away too, is that it?"

"We just want you to be... *careful*."

"Or what? I'll find a mini-bus outside the house to take me and the family to Scarborough? Is that how you deal with your known agitators now is it? I tell you what. Instead of wasting your time with all this nonsense why don't you do something useful and get rid of those bloody hippies who have taken over Llys Meifor instead?"

The Londoner suddenly gripped The Hangman's arm and dug his fingers so hard into his flesh it felt as if they were touching the bone. The Hangman wanted to yell out in pain but his pride wouldn't allow it. There were tears in his eyes.

"Take it easy," said the Londoner, his voice now a growl. "Behave yourself. Be a good boy for two weeks and that way no one gets hurt."

THIRTY FOUR

When Miriam had been a child back in Pantglyn she had stood up to sing on tip-toe in chapel. She had been in the company of giants and had shouted out hymns to make sure God heard her although she had often wondered if God had really needed to be reminded how great he was once a week. If he knew everything then surely he knew that too?

People just didn't believe anymore. In just a little under ten years, centuries of faith had popped like a soap bubble. Each Sunday, there were rows of empty pews in Bethel chapel and the unbelievers were seen around the village during the rest of the week entirely unconcerned by the prospect of God's wrath. What would poor old Gladys have thought of it all? If she came back from the dead tomorrow she would assume she had landed on an alien planet! Even her precious Llys Meifor was gone – or, at least, gone as she had known it. The shell of the house was there, sold to a man from Liverpool over the phone at an auction – a man who had never even been over to see it. Now it had fallen into disrepair and had been taken over by a bunch of hippies who tried to sell their terrible pottery from the front garden to whoever was passing by.

In the bathroom mirror Miriam stretched the skin and imagined what she would look like with one of those facelifts the film stars sometimes had. But there was no point because they cost hundreds of pounds and she couldn't afford it. Ordinary people like her didn't get facelifts. They just had to put up with the fact that they were getting old. Nine years had slipped by as swiftly and as sneakily as weasels since the day she had moved to Bethel from Pantglyn. Now, approaching thirty, she tried to see at least a trace of that young girl staring back at her from the other side of the mirror – the young girl in her bedroom with the frilly lampshade and the books about ballerinas who had dreamt of a life of travel and romance and excitement. She sometimes thought that she had caught a fleeting glimpse and, when she did, she touched the cold glass with her fingers in the hope that it might somehow melt like syrup and allow her to slip through like Alice.

The letter had arrived that morning. Miriam had picked it up along with the small pile of bills and, spotting the familiar handwriting on the envelope – and then the Dublin postmark – all the air was suddenly sucked out of her lungs and she felt she was going to faint. She leant against the wall and tried to recover but there was no time because she could hear Daniel coming out of the bathroom and soon he would be running down the stairs looking for his briefcase which contained all the marked homework from last night. Miriam had stuffed the letter up her jumper. When Daniel came down the stairs he asked her what was wrong but she just smiled sweetly and said she was fine. She had even kissed him on the cheek. Which Daniel had clearly thought was a bit odd.

Now, a couple of hours later and alone in the house, Miriam sat at the kitchen table and stared at the still unopened letter. She picked it up once more and felt it with her fingers and thumbs, digging her nails into the paper until they made tiny, arc-like indentations. It was thick. Pages upon pages of his folded up handwriting telling her all about his new life. Had he got married? Were there any children? Did he make them straw bobbies in the garden and make them laugh? Whatever he was up to he was clearly still thinking of her and she hadn't been forgotten. She placed the letter down again and went over to the window to stop herself from opening it. Life had moved on. Opening the letter would have been like placing her hands on that cold glass. There was no way back. It was a life that had never happened.

THIRTY FIVE

Leah now lived in Bethel too. She had moved in to one of the new council houses with Cerwyn and her son Llew. Although it wasn't like the old days in poor Mr Oliver's shop when they had been giggly and silly and living in each other's pockets they still made time for each other and usually met on Thursday mornings for tea, biscuits and a gossip in their respective houses. That week it was Miriam's turn.

"We're being followed."

"What?"

Leah placed her tea down.

"Well, *Cerwyn's* being followed at any rate. There's a car outside the house night and day with these two men in it and they're watching the house."

"What for?"

"Oh I don't know. He's always shooting his mouth off isn't he? You know what he's like. Flying off the handle. I'll be glad when all this Investiture nonsense is all over. Then this place can go back to normal."

She picked up her mug, blew away some steam and sipped it thoughtfully.

"He thinks the world of Daniel you know."

"Does he?"

Leah nodded.

"Talks about him all the time. He's doing well isn't he?"

Miriam sat down opposite her friend.

"I hardly ever see him," she said, with a mock roll of her eyes. "He's either upstairs in his study working on another of his poems or in the garden playing football with the boy."

"How many eisteddfod chairs has he won now?"

"Too many! We've had to give some of them away. If you're short of chairs in the house let me know! But it's the big one he wants."

Leah nodded.

"The National."

"Three times he's tried. He came close last year though. Second apparently."

"Wouldn't that be great?" said Leah wistfully. "Having a proper bardic poet as a husband! You'd be like the Queen! Queen Miriam the First!"

They laughed.

"You know what today is don't you?" said Leah. "It's eleven years since I first met Cerwyn in The Britannia. Do you remember? That night it was raining so hard and we had to run and you let me win?"

Miriam sipped her tea.

"I remember."

"It was the most exciting thing. Stuff like that never happened to me! I was always the ugly one so when he popped the question right there and then, well, I didn't know what to think! I thought he was joking!"

"But he wasn't."

"No," said Leah, "thankfully."

They both smiled. But then Leah's smile evaporated. She put down her tea and leant forward.

"Are you alright?"

"What do you mean?"

"There's just this faraway look in your eyes. You're not pregnant are you?"

"Hell no!"

Miriam lifted her mug but didn't drink. She placed it back on the table and looked at Leah, although Leah noticed that she couldn't keep eye contact for very long. Miriam sighed.

"I don't know what it is," she said. "I've got a nice life and everything what with Daniel and the boy and this house. But do you ever get this feeling that..."

"What?"

"Oh nothing."

"No tell me!"

Miriam looked at her friend and sighed again.

"Well, I just sometimes get this odd feeling that something terrible is going to happen to me and all of this might be taken away. Something really bad."

After Leah had gone Miriam picked up the letter from Dublin. She ran her thumbnail along the edge, almost daring herself to open it. But she didn't.

She ran up the stairs, took out the little step-ladder, climbed up and opened the hatch to the attic. Remembering only to stand on the wooden beams – like the builder had advised when they'd first moved in – Miriam edged along carefully until she reached the boxes in the far corner. One of them was overflowing with Christmas decorations. Another held the artificial tree. Next to them were some boxes containing some of John and Gladys's old things – photo albums and various bits and pieces but then – tucked away almost out of sight – there was the plastic bag containing an old shoe box. Miriam picked it up, blew away the cobwebs and opened it for the first time in years. It contained all the letters

Pádraig had sent her while she'd been young and foolish and full of dreams. She raised the box to her nose and the letters smelled mouldy and decayed. The life they documented was ancient history, wads tied up with elastic bands like currency that was no longer tenable. Miriam took the unopened letter from her pocket and quickly stuffed it in next to the others before she changed her mind. One day she would take the letter out and read it. When she was ready.

THIRTY SIX

Moonglow smelled of flowers. Sometimes it was so strong that when I stood too close to him I felt I was going to sneeze. Moonglow's father smelled of flowers too. And his mother. All the hippies at Llys Meifor smelled like flowers. Standing next to them was like standing in a field. I hadn't meant to go back to Llys Meifor. My Dad had told me to stay well clear because there were probably drugs there. Some of the hippies walked around naked, he said. I couldn't imagine anybody going out naked in Bethel. Not even in mid-June. But I was always curious about the hippies. And that was how I got caught. I was suddenly tapped on the shoulder and, turning round, I saw a smiling boy about my age. His hair was long and thick.

"Hi, my name's Moonglow, " he said. "I'm the son of Wandering Elk. Do you want to see my wigwam?"

He didn't even bother to wait for my answer. He grabbed me by the arm and led me round the side of Llys Meifor – past a group of long-haired and bearded half-naked men who were fixing a battered old Bedford van whilst listening to some pop music on a tinny radio. We walked past the door where, long ago, my great-grandfather had once held his surgeries. Now the door had been painted over in a rainbow design.

I followed Moonglow into the back garden. It wasn't how I remembered it. Now it was almost completely overgrown, the bushes were as wild as monsters and the grass was so long it had about three colours – green, yellow and dull grey. Some of the blades were as long as sabres.

"Down here," said Moonglow.

We walked past the wooden bench where only a few years earlier I'd sat with Nain before she died. I wondered if the little
carving was still there – the one Bethel Taid had once made for
her with his pocket knife – but we were moving too quickly so I
couldn't check. The pond had dried up. It was a dark brown bath
tub. Then, on the other side, rising out of the tall grass like a
cream-coloured triangle, I saw the wigwam.

"My Dad made it for me," said Moonglow. "He says they're
not really called 'wigwams'. He says that's just what we call them.
They should be called teepees."

"What does your Dad do?" I asked.

Moonglow shrugged.

"He tells stories. Want to see inside?"

He opened the flap and I followed him. There was a mud-
spattered rug on the floor and we both sat down.

"I've got a Calumet."

Moonglow reached into a tatty old box and took out a long
pipe which had been painted in bright colours.

"You're allowed to smoke?"

"Not really," said Moonglow. "I will when I'm older though.
But I can sit around the fire when the elders do it and pretend."

"My friend Llew smokes sometimes. He steals one of his Dad's
cigarettes."

Moonglow placed the pipe back in the box.

"Want to see something really special? Look. This is my
medicine bag."

Out of his pocket he'd taken out a pouch which was made of
soft leather.

"What does it do?"

"It protects me."

"From what?"

"From anything. Dad says the old Human Beings – that's the Indians in America – took their medicine bags into battle so that they wouldn't be hurt by guns or arrows. Want to hold it?"

He handed me the pouch. I felt it between my fingers.

"Can I open it?"

Moonglow shook his head gravely.

"My Dad says that once the bag's been tied up it becomes sacred. If you open it up then all the Aura will seep out."

"What's an aura?"

"The Aura is what makes you powerful. It's the thing that protects you."

"Like a shield?" I said.

Moonglow thought about it.

"Yeah, I suppose so."

"Can anyone get the aura?"

"Think so. Why? Do you want it? My Dad can give it to you if you want. There's a ceremony you have to go through but it's no problem. I can ask him."

THIRTY SEVEN

Roughly halfway up the winding path, overlooking a gully which was said to have been gouged out of the rock by Henllyn – the enormous eagle of ancient Welsh mythology – there sat the White Lady.

"There she is boys," said T.J. Watcyn, clambering up to the very edge and trying to disguise his breathlessness. "The White Lady. We're still safe!"

As a boy Daniel had been told the story of Henllyn many times. How the fearsome eagle had ripped out a piece of the mountain to feed its young so that they would grow up to be strong and fearless in the face of enemies. The hole that remained was said to go all the way down to the centre of the world. That was why the White Lady had appeared, the last act of magic ever known in Wales. She had come out of the stone overlooking the gully to warn passers-by of the danger. The legend also said that, if the White Lady ever crumbled and fell down the bottomless pit, then Wales would fall down with her.

Stepping as close as he dared to the brink, Daniel jolted as T.J. Watcyn slapped a hand on his shoulder. The old bard nodded in the direction of the strange, chalk-like marks in the rock on the other side of the abyss.

"Doesn't look much like a lady does it? Believe that bollocks do you?"

"I'm... not sure."

T.J Watcyn grunted and took his hand away from Daniel's

shoulder.

"A geological freak," he said. "That's what we've placed our faith in. An accident of nature. The English wouldn't believe this crap about a White Lady. They were always too busy conquering the world. Unsentimental and unimaginative bastards the lot of them but who needs imagination when you've got India? Eh boy? The ones with imagination are always the losers. They worry too much. Spend all their lives dreaming. Like us Welsh, writing cynghanedd whilst the colonists fuck our daughters."

"They want hanging," said Cerwyn Evans. "I'd hang the bloody lot of them; the Queen, the Duke of Edinburgh, the Queen Mother and all the little princes and princesses. In public too!"

"I can just imagine you in your black hood," said John Tŷ Mawr, smiling and winking at Trefor Rowland and Rhydian Vaughan. "Pulling that lever on the entire House of Windsor."

"The Hangman," said T.J. Watcyn. "That's what we should call you."

The others all laughed, even Daniel allowed himself a smile, but The Hangman didn't see the joke.

"What he needs is a wife," said Rhydian Vaughan.

John Tŷ Mawr sniggered.

"Who'd take him though?"

"I could get a wife anytime I wanted," said The Hangman. "I could get one tonight if I wanted to!"

"A fiver says you can't," said Trefor Rowlands.

The Hangman leered at him and at all the others in turn.

"You're on," he said.

THIRTY EIGHT

Wandering Elk had cleared a space in the middle of Llys Meifor's lounge to make room for the Aura ceremony. There was a bowl of water at his feet and he was holding a tambourine which looked a bit like the one we had at school only this one had colourful ribbons tied to it. On his head was a magnificent bonnet with a twin trail of feathers which almost reached the ground.

"Which one is to receive the Aura?" he said.

I pushed Llew forward because he was too scared to step forward himself.

"It's okay," whispered Moonglow to him. "It doesn't hurt."

"The Aura is a special and mysterious gift," intoned Wandering Elk, closing his eyes and stretching out his arms like Jesus. "Given down through the ages from one tribal elder to another and then shared among their people by medicine men and shamen, it has been a sacred power since the time when Human Beings first walked on the earth." He opened his eyes again and fixed them on Llew. "Do you understand?"

Llew nodded.

"It is not a power to be shared lightly," intoned Wandering Elk, closing his eyes again. "It is to be respected and revered. The Aura can be a protection against illness and disease, against ignorance and wilfulness, against the extremities of the elements and also against the forces of violence. But remember, it must never be used to instigate violence."

Wandering Elk knelt down, dipped his fingers in the bowl of

water and, stretching up to his full height again, he took a deep breath and sprinkled the water in Llew's face whilst chanting something that sounded like nonsense. Wandering Elk and all the other hippies in had their eyes tightly closed though so I presumed it to be some sort of serious prayer. Even the dog stopped licking his bum and sat up, his ears stiff as sticks.

Wandering Elk took something out of the pockets of his jeans and handed it to Llew.

"This is your special medicine bag," he said. "What's your name?"

"Llew. "

"Well now you have a new name. Now you are Proud Pony."

Wandering Elk flicked some more water in Llew's face and then he clapped his hands. It was all over. The other hippies stood up and began to move things back into the centre of the floor again and the dog carried on licking his bum.

"Do you feel different?" asked Moonglow, clearly excited.

"Not really," said Llew

"Well, sometimes it takes a while."

Llew looked at the small medicine bag dubiously.

"You sure this works?"

Moonglow smiled.

"Did for me."

"They're going to kidnap us," said Llew.

It was half an hour later and we were sitting outside the village shop.

"Who?"

"MI5. They've been parked outside our house. Dad said they would take us all away until the Investiture was over just in case Dad blew up Prince Charles with the Free Wales Army."

I stopped chewing my Twix.

"Is your Dad in the Free Wales Army?"

Llew shook his head.

"He just knows people who are. And then he's been writing all those stupid poems and letters. He's dead jealous of your Dad. Mum told me."

"Why?"

"Because he writes better poems."

"Why would anyone be jealous about poems?"

Llew shrugged. Out on the main road an army truck thundered by full of soldiers. It had been exciting to look at them when they'd first driven through the village but now no one bothered to go out and wave.

"Where will they take you?" I asked.

But Llew just shrugged again.

"I think they were just trying to scare him."

He turned to me with a wary look in his eye.

"Is he your new mate now?"

"Who?"

"That hippie."

"I hardly know him. He just showed me round because I used to live there."

Llew took the little leather pouch out of his jeans pocket. He rubbed it with his finger and thumb.

"Doesn't feel very magical."

"You feeling different yet?"

Llew shook his head. He closed his eyes tightly as if he was concentrating really hard on something. Behind me I heard voices and I recognised Farming Boy and his gang walking across the field path towards the village shop.

"Maybe we should go," I said.

But Llew didn't move.

"Hang on," he said, his eyes still closed. "There's definitely something. A weird kind of tingling."

Farming Boy spotted us. I tugged Llew's arm but he wasn't budging. His eyes were closed tight like two minus signs.

"It's like my bones are becoming steel."

"Steel eh?" said Farming Boy.

Llew opened his eyes and saw Farming Boy and his gang but he didn't seem scared or worried at all.

"It's the Aura," he said.

Farming Boy snorted. He turned to his mates. Then back to Llew.

"You taking the piss?"

"Let's go," I said, hopping off the wall and trying to take Llew with me. But Llew was as heavy as a bear.

"It's okay," he said.

"Lick my boot you little fucker."

Even though it was summer, Farming Boy was wearing his huge Doctor Martens. Now his left foot was raised.

"No," said Llew calmly. "I'm not scared of you anymore."

Farming Boy brought down his left foot and took a step closer. Pushing me out of the way as if I didn't matter in his world he started kicking Llew from all directions. Every kick had a different sound, like a variety of drums being struck and Farming Boy made sure that his Doctor Marten's smashed into as many parts of Llew's body as possible. The kicking went on and on and no one stopped it. No one came out of the shop. No one drove by. Some birds sang up on the electricity wires above my head and it didn't seem right. Then, at last, Farming Boy stopped kicking. He wiped the side of his mouth and stepped back where his mates laughed and congratulated him on a good job. Scraping the back of his throat he brought up a mouthful of phlegm, leant over Llew's crumpled body and allowed the green ball to dangle on a glistening, web-thin line of spit before landing it onto Llew's hair. Then, just for good measure, he gave him one final kick in the stomach.

"Little cunt."

The following day I gave Llew my gun.

THIRTY NINE

As a child, Daniel had been fascinated by Llanddeiniolen ceme-tery which lay two miles outside Bethel on a windswept hill. The older graves were grim and forbidding slate rectangles covered in moss and lichen. Nobody knew who was inside anymore. All the relatives, the sons and daughters and grandchildren – even the great-grandchildren – had all died too and there was no one left to scour the stuff away to reveal the carved letters or dates. Was he going to lie dead in a grave one day too? Long gone and forgotten? He couldn't imagine it. He was too strong. Too young. But the young died too.

The grave that had intrigued him most was a simple one tucked up against the very walls of Llanddeiniolen church itself. He'd been attracted by the plastic toy windmill that someone had stuck on it. It had rattled in the breeze as he'd sat on a wall waiting for Gladys and John to finish whatever boring stuff they were doing and, because it seemed that they would take forever about it, he had hopped off the wall for a closer look.

The plastic windmill caught the breeze intermittently, the bright colours of its blades merging into a white circle before slowing down again as if it had been caught doing something it shouldn't. Someone had also left a packet of Dolly Mixtures on the grave. He tried to read the letters on the gravestone but centuries of rough weather had scrubbed them away.

On the way home he asked Gladys about it and she said the grave had been that of a young girl who had died hundreds of years ago. Some people still left sweets and toys for her, she said, so that she could eat and play in heaven.

He felt stupid but there was no one around so he walked over to the side of the church and knelt down beside the little girl's grave. Someone had been round recently because a childish and rather withered bunch of violets and buttercups had been thrown down on the grave. Daniel looked over his shoulder. The place was quiet. A cow mooed in the distance and a bee sawed through the air. Another army truck full of soldiers rumbled by on its way to the Investiture preparations in Caernarfon but, after that, there was nothing. Not even a breeze. Not a cloud in the sky.

He reached into his pocket and took out the packet of Jelly Tots he'd bought in the garage along with the flowers. He ripped open the packet with his teeth and poured the sugared jellies onto the grave. They glistened in the sunlight like imitation diamonds. Then, behind him, a voice.

"Lovely afternoon."

Daniel jolted as if someone had poked him in the back. Turning round he patted the sugar from his hands and saw a woman. She was around the same age as himself, possibly a few years older, and was wearing a bright yellow dress. She was holding some flowers and a trowel.

"Yes," he said, realizing that it had taken him too long to reply. "Yes, lovely."

The woman smiled and walked off. Had she seen him drop the sweets on the grave? Did she think he was some kind of maniac? He swept his hand through his hair and straightened his tie. Up ahead he saw the woman in the yellow dress turning to the left. Relieved, Daniel walked along the path and turned to the right towards Gladys and John's grave.

When Gladys had died just a year or so earlier Daniel had commissioned a new headstone to include both his parents' names together with an image of two hands locked in prayer. It shone beautifully, untarnished by weeds, ivy or lichen. He took the wilted flowers out of the pot and replaced them with the new ones, arranging them inexpertly. Miriam would have done a better job. He knew that. He wiped his hands.

"You know I was never one for flowers Mum," he said. "But I bought these. I hope you like them. Dad, I hope you feel happier now that Mum is there with you."

Were they there? Could they hear him?

He cleared his throat and smiled.

"Ramsay seems pretty cocky about his chances of retaining the World Cup next year Dad," he said. "Mind you, the heat in Mexico could be a problem. I hope they get hammered. Too big for their boots I reckon. They could do with being brought down a peg or two!"

But then his face became more serious.

"They're closing the quarry Dad. It's been on the cards for a while. There's only a handful of men working there now and they've got a machine to do what you did. It can slice the slate perfectly every time apparently."

A big dragonfly landed on the gravestone, wiggled its antennae for a few seconds and then took off again.

"Those hippies are still in Llys Meifor, Mum. But as soon as this Investiture is over the talk is that the police will move them on. It was a mistake to sell the place to that man from Liverpool. He's never been round once."

He checked his watch.

"I'd better go. Miriam will have prepared tea. But I'll be back. To keep you up to date with things."

Aware that the dead were watching him but knowing also that they told no tales Daniel chucked the wilted flowers over the wall into the next field and wiped his hands. The new flowers looked pretty. Wiping his hands on his trousers he left the graveside but, instead of heading back along the path towards the lane where he'd parked the Cortina, he glanced across to the far side of the cemetery. He hadn't paid his respects to T.J. Watcyn for a while and he felt guilty.

He strolled along the narrow path and was surprised to see that the woman in the yellow dress that he'd spoken to earlier was kneeling over the great bard's grave. Hearing footsteps approaching, she turned round. She smiled and Daniel finally remembered where he'd seen her before. At the funeral four years earlier. She was Catrin. T.J.'s daughter.

"We meet again," she said.

"I'm sorry," said Daniel. "I didn't recognise you. Earlier I mean. From the... from the funeral."

Catrin stood up and polished the top of the gravestone with a cloth.

"Yes well, he was always the star wasn't he? The one everyone noticed. I suppose it was to be expected. Me and my Mum were always in his shadow." She tucked the cloth in her bag and turned to Daniel. "He often used to talk about you."

"Really?"

Catrin nodded thoughtfully.

"He said you were the only one of his students who had genuine talent. He said you could win the crown or the chair at the National Eisteddfod one day."

"Well, it hasn't happened."

"It didn't for him either at first," said Catrin, glancing back at the grave and then smiling sadly. "Drove my poor Mum mad. I think that's when the trouble started to be honest. She wanted him to win just so that it would all stop. But of course, him winning was the worst thing that could have happened."

"I'm afraid I don't..."

"Drink. Old story I'm afraid. I know more about it now. All that expectation that was suddenly on his shoulders. The fear that he'd fooled everyone and that he'd never write a great poem again. That idea that he was a fraud." She shook her head. "He'd throw things around – pots, chairs, plates. Finally, punches and kicks."

"I had no idea."

"Oh, he was a good actor," said Catrin, turning to Daniel with a sardonic smile. "Up there with the likes of Burton. Playing the part of The Great Bard. The role he was born to play!" She looked down at the grave again and lowered her voice. "I was only little. So I used to hide in the wardrobe. I had to promise to tell everyone that my mother was the clumsiest woman in Caernarfon. How she kept walking into doors. Falling down stairs."

During the awkward pause Daniel thought of taking a step forward but he didn't. He thought of saying something. But he couldn't think what.

Catrin looked directly at him.

"I saw you putting sweets on Little Anna's grave earlier."

"I... er..."

"It's okay. I've done it myself before now."

"Anna. Was that her name?"

Catrin shrugged.

"It's what my father always called her. He told me that he remembered her being called Little Anna when he was a boy."

"What happened to her?"

"Who knows?" said Catrin with a sigh as she gathered up her things and put them back in the plastic bag. "Some say it was the plague. Others that she was the daughter of a local witch." She laughed gently. "Such silly stories. Anyway, it's been nice talking to you but I should be going. The bus is due."

"I can offer you a lift if you like."

"You're very kind," said Catrin. "But it's fine."

FORTY

The Hangman had knocked back pints at twice his normal rate and now The Britannia swayed like an old clipper on the Irish Sea. This nautical effect was enhanced by the rain which whipped against the windows and by the waves caused by the buses as they sloshed their way along the road outside towards Caernarfon Maes. Realising that he'd lost the thread of the conversation John Tŷ Mawr, Rhydian Vaughan and Trefor Rowlands were having with the new boy Daniel, The Hangman stood up and peered through the clear glass at the top of the window and watched the passengers disembarking from the buses – the gaberdined men holding on to their hats and the women shrieking under snapping umbrellas. Then he took a messy mouthful of beer and sat down again. He leant across the table, pinning them all with his eyes.

"I could get a woman if I wanted."

They stopped talking and looked at him.

"What are you on about now?" said John Tŷ Mawr, laughing.

"The old man," said The Hangman, nodding to his left as if T.J. Watcyn was actually in the room. "This morning up the mountain. He said he'd be impressed if I got a wife. Well I could get a wife. I could get one tonight."

Rhydian Vaughan sniggered.

"You're drunk."

The Hangman stuck up two fingers at him. He gulped some more beer.

"I need fresh air."

Could he be honest with himself now? Now that there was only himself standing in the doorway of The Britannia holding his near-empty glass? Could he admit that he was actually jealous? He'd been the best once. Not brilliant. But the old man had grunted a concession that he sometimes managed a reasonable couplet in perfect cynghanedd and that was as good as it got – a nod and an appreciative look. Until that little bastard came along with his swept back hair and doe eyes. His first session and T.J. gives him something better than a grunt. He gives him a look he'd never seen before. A look signifying that maybe he was something special.

The Hangman watched as a Crossville bus stopped in the middle of the Maes. The rain was relentless. Behind him, inside The Britannia, someone had started a singalong – the out of tune piano crashing out discordant clangs. He watched as a girl in a red dress came out of the Crossville bus desperately trying to protect her hairdo. She needn't have bothered. Even from that distance The Hangman reckoned that she was probably the ugliest girl he had ever seen. But the one she ran up to was a perfect angel – so beautiful and elegant as she laughed and tried to shield her ugly friend's hair from the weather. He assumed that they were going to make a dash for the Castle Arms but no, the angel was pointing in the direction of The Britannia. They started running. As she did so the angel looked up and, for a second or two, she caught The Hangman's eye. Her ugly friend was trying to catch up but it was no good. She was too slow and heavy. The angel was leaving her behind and heading straight towards The Hangman like a gift from heaven.

"I've just seen her."

"Who?" said Rhydian Vaughan, winking mischievously at the others, "Sophia Loren?"

But The Hangman didn't smile. He sat down. Then he stood up. He was breathless. He ran his hand through his hair and straightened his collar. Looked at the door. Then at the others.

"The girl I'm going to marry."

John Tŷ Mawr laughed.

"You must be more pissed than I thought," he said. "Someone get him another pint for God's sake, before he declares himself the King of Wales or something."

The Hangman suddenly lunged across the table and snatched him by the lapel.

"That's the thing with you isn't it?" he snarled. "You think I'm a joke. You think everything's a fucking joke!"

"Bloody hell mate. Cool it!"

The Hangman released his grip and pushed him away.

"T.J. said I should get a wife and that's what I'm going to do."

"He wasn't being serious," said Trefor Rowland. "He was just teasing you."

"Who's the lucky lady? Anyone we know?"

John Tŷ Mawr hid his smirk behind his pint. He winked at Daniel but Daniel was too new and too polite to wink back.

"Five pounds," said The Hangman. "Five pounds says I'll go up and offer to buy her a drink. The next woman to walk through that door."

"I thought you were going to marry her," said Rhydian Vaughan.

"I'll do that too."

"You're an idiot," said John Tŷ Mawr.

"Put your money where that smug mouth of yours is and we'll see."

"Okay boys," said John Tŷ Mawr, reaching into his pocket. "Let's chip in. Let's put a fiver down and see this clown make a fool of himself."

The Hangman smiled, and kept his eye on the door.

"Wait till you see her," he said.

The choir in the far corner lunged into another indistinct Irish tune and some of the onlookers in The Britannia joined in even though they seemed to neither know nor care how the original melody went. Everyone was in full voice as the door of the Britannia opened and Leah staggered in, her red dress soaking. Breathless. Her curls a mess.

FORTY ONE

"It's not real," I said.

"Looks real."

"I know. But it doesn't shoot bullets. It shoots pellets. It's an air pistol. Pantglyn Taid gave it to me and said I should keep it a secret."

Llew weighed the pistol in his hand.

"So is it loaded?"

I gave him a doubtful look. I was beginning to wonder whether this had been a good idea. Llew took aim at a tree trunk. He pulled the trigger and the pellet shot out in a flash of silver before it was caught by the breeze and dropped harmlessly in the grass about fifty yards away.

"Wow! It really works!"

He tucked the pistol in his jeans and pulled down his jumper to hide it as best he could.

Nansi Dodd was smoking a fag and giggling. She was pretty. Far too pretty for Farming Boy. But somehow she'd agreed to go out with him. Now he wanted to show her how powerful he was. He found us on the swing.

"There's my slave!" he shouted, unhooking himself from Nansi Dodd. "Hey slave! Lick my boots!"

"I'm not your slave," said Llew.

"You little shit."

He acted annoyed but I sensed that Farming Boy was relishing the chance to show off in front of his new girlfriend. Running over he picked Llew up and dragged him like a sack across to the wire fence, pushing him against it until it crashed like a cymbal. Despite the noise no one came to help. The windows of the new council houses overlooking the playground were as blank and uncomprehending as the eyes of cats. Farming Boy kneed Llew in the face. There was a small cracking sound, like when you stepped on the skull of a dead bird on the beach. He did it again. Then once more. When he stepped away I saw that Llew's entire face was red. Farming Boy kicked him in the chest and then drove the heel of his boot hard into his bollocks. He picked Llew up by the hair and forced him up unsteadily on his feet.

"Go over there and lick her shoe."

Nansi Dodd grimaced.

"Fuck off," she said. "I don't want his blood all over my shoe!"

With the blood still pumping from his nose, Llew broke into a red smile. He took the air pistol out of his jeans and shot Farming Boy in the eye.

FORTY TWO

"Come down! We know you're up there!"

The policeman was standing at the bottom of the tree holding a megaphone.

"Either you can come down or we can climb up. It's up to you."

Llew grabbed my arm.

"You won't leave me up here will you?"

We were about twenty feet above ground and I didn't like it. The slightest breeze caused the branches to sway and I felt I was on a horrible fairground ride. Down below, through the mass of leaves, I saw the two policemen. Behind them, a small crowd had gathered. Soon it would be the whole of the village.

"Do you think I killed him?"

"It's only an air pistol. I told you."

"But it was close range. What if it went all the way into his brain?"

I'd never seen Llew looking so scared. I thought he was going to cry. The megaphone crackled again twenty feet below us.

"This is your final warning. Do you understand me boys?"

"We can't stay here forever," I said.

"I'll go to jail. Or borstal!"

"I'll say it was an accident."

"What about that girl? She'll say I deliberately shot him in the face! And she'd be right!"

There had been an ambulance. We had heard it about five or

ten minutes after the shooting – while we were desperately trying to find somewhere to hide. I had imagined Farming Boy speeding towards the Caernarfon and Anglesey Hospital with sirens wailing and with a blood-soaked bandage over his eyes.

"It'll be tea-time soon," I said. "My Dad will come home."

Llew tightened his grip on my arm.

"*You can't leave me!*"

Down below someone had found a ladder and it was being leant up against the tree trunk and steadied. As the top of the ladder poked in to our private world, Llew backed away but the branch he was sitting on became thinner and less able to support his weight. Then, like something out of a panto, the head of a stranger peeped in to the magical green world. His walkie-talkie crackled.

"Okay lads," he said, in a tough London accent. "You've had your fun. But now it's time to come down."

FORTY THREE

Prince Charles looked nervous. He knew they were watching. Not just the people in Caernarfon castle – the soldiers and the bands and the dignitaries – but also all those anonymous millions who were watching him on telly. From Timbuctoo to Tokyo, all eyes were on tiny Caernarfon. We were watching too. Three miles away in Bethel. In The Hangman's house.

Llew had asked me to go to his house (even though they only had a black and white TV and ours was in colour) because his probation officer was with him and she hadn't finished filling in his forms yet. There had been rumours of borstal – mainly from Farming Boy's family who had told everyone they met that they hoped to see Llew being carted off in a Black Maria to the outskirts of Liverpool or Manchester and never seen again until he was a sad and broken old man of seventy – but the probation officer had a kind face and she kept telling Llew and his Mum and Dad that everything would be alright.

The MI5 guys were there too, sitting forward politely on the ragged sofa by the window (the curtains having been drawn because the bright sunlight made the television screen hard to see). They ate chocolate digestives and sipped tea from Investiture mugs. The one with the London accent winked at me sometimes as if he'd found grabbing a pair of felons from a tree to be quite funny. I'd expected The Hangman to be angry that we were watching the Investiture but he didn't seem bothered. He wasn't drinking tea though. He was on his third whiskey.

"Soon be over boys," he said, addressing the two MI5 guys. "Then you can go back to London and be little James Bonds again."

One of them leant across to one side on the sofa to get a better view of the screen.

"Reckon J5 is on point?"

"Probably. At junction twelve."

The first MI5 guy nodded solemnly. He checked his watch and nodded in the direction of the screen.

"Should be merging with the mountain crew now."

"Like clockwork those guys."

Leah came in with more biscuits and tea.

"Oh dear," she said, looking at the screen. "That's a terrible picture. Hold this tray Llew. Let's see if we can sort this aerial out." She turned to The Hangman and glanced disapprovingly at the whisky. "Are you going to help me?"

But The Hangman suddenly spat at the screen. It landed like a blob of silver in the middle of Prince Charles's forehead and dribbled all the way down his nervous face. Then the shot changed and it crawled down one of the towers towards the cheering crowds.

"You filthy pig!" said Leah. "Clean that up right away!"

"*You* clean it! I'm going out to the shed for some bloody peace!"

The MI5 guys looked at each other. The first one nodded after The Hangman and the second one sighed heavily. He shoved half a chocolate digestive in his mouth and stood up to follow The Hangman. Just to be sure.

FORTY FOUR

Once the Investiture was over Bethel returned to normal. Bunting and flags were taken down from the lamposts and cars no longer had to avoid piles of horseshit on the main road to Caernarfon.

Farming Boy came out of hospital wearing a flesh-coloured eye-patch which the doctors had said he had to keep on for a month until his eye got better.

I had to confess that it had been my air pistol that had been used to shoot him and my Mum told me off for hiding it upstairs in my drawer.

Three weeks later the *Caernarfon and Denbigh Herald* published one of The Hangman's poems again. It was about Prince Charles being mauled by a dragon.

FORTY FIVE

Inflatable Santas had been stuffed into shop windows, multi-coloured light-bulbs hung on trees, brass bands huddled together for warmth on Caernarfon's Maes and the ancient castle walls were made jolly by a wash of bright yellow lights. It seemed to Miriam as if Christmas came earlier each year. As a kid it had seemed to have taken forever to arrive. She had pestered Alwyn and Eluned for a pen so that she could write her letter to Father Christmas telling him how much she would have loved to have a musical jewellery box with a dancing ballerina inside it like the one she'd seen in Nelson's shop window in Caernarfon but they had shooed her away telling her it was too early. Now she was older. The months sped by. Christmas was just under a month away. And she had no money. In her purse there were three pound notes and some shillings and pence and that had to last for another week. Out of that she needed to buy the food, a new school blazer for the boy (after he'd ripped it on a nail) and a pair of knickers for herself. Sometimes she went without – even on cold November days – whilst the two pairs she had left were in the wash. She felt the draught up her inner thighs and instinctively drew her legs together in case a sudden gale caught her unawares.

The boy had already shown her the letter he was going to send up to the North Pole – a side of foolscap written in his best handwriting using the fountain pen he'd borrowed from his Dad. Top of the list, inevitably – and underlined this time in slightly smudged blue ink – was a GI Action Gun. Every time the advert came on the TV Miriam was aware of his silent, pleading gaze but she always pretended not to notice. They both knew that Daniel had always made it clear that there would be no toy guns in the house, just like he did every year. This year however, after the incident with Farming Boy and Llew, the rule was even more stringently expressed than ever. Besides, the GI Action Gun cost a thumping two pounds. More than the cost of a turkey.

Miriam had felt sorry for the boy. She identified with the pleading look. It had been the same with her ballerina jewellery box. There had been no TV adverts back then but how many times had she opened and closed the little jewellery box in Nelson's when she was a little girl, sticking her ear as close as she could to the plastic ballerina to hear the tinkling music above the noise of the people in the shop? She had no idea. But she guessed it would have been as many times as Eluned had dragged her away because their bus back home to Pantglyn had just pulled in to Caernarfon Maes. She had been yanked away from the haughty ballerina (who had always seemed so serene and so unconcerned with the chaos of life around her) but the young Miriam had always looked back, hoping that one day she would wake up on Christmas morning to the delicious surprise of finding it in her stocking. She never did. For years she blamed Father Christmas for being too stupid to understand her Welsh handwriting. She should have used English instead. It was only later, when she'd left her childhood behind, that she'd realised that the precious box had been nineteen shillings – more than Eluned or Alwyn could possibly have afforded.

Across the Maes people were crowding in and out of buses and, from the Castle Arms, she could hear a rowdy and somewhat drunken rendition of 'Good King Wenceslas.' She was only yards away from the spot where Daniel had almost run her over a little more than ten years earlier. Somebody in the council must have realised that it was a dangerous spot because now there was a small barrier and some traffic lights to protect the unwary pedestrian. Had there been traffic lights and a barrier back then would she be in Ireland by now living life as a good Catholic wife with Pádraig? How many children would she have? Six? Eight? Ten?

The letter had never been opened. It was still up there in the attic. Maybe he had forgotten about her now, given her up. He would have known what had happened. Eluned would have written to him and asked him not to get in touch because it was probably for the best now that she had a new life, a new husband. A child. She did think about him though. That shock of unruly ginger hair that was always flopping down over his forehead and that semi-permanent smile which seemed to suggest that everything was always going to be fine – that life was a breeze and that resistance was futile. Did he still look the same? Maybe he'd got fat. Or bald. Maybe he'd lost a tooth. Or his religion. Ten years was a long time. Anything could happen.

"Bugger it."

She walked into Nelson's, past the huge Christmas tree in the front door, past the glistening bottles of perfume where once the dancing ballerina had mesmerised her and straight up the stairs to the toy department. She whipped two pounds from her purse and asked the assistant for the GI Action Gun.

She watched as the assistant wrapped it. It wasn't too late to say no. The box was much bigger than she'd anticipated. It would be almost impossible to hide until Christmas. It wasn't too late to say no. She held the two pounds in her hand. The assistant placed the box on the counter. It wasn't too late to say no. How would she explain to Daniel that she'd run out of money? And what would she say on Christmas morning when the boy would squeal with joy and insist on showing him what Santa had left? The assistant smiled expectantly. Miriam handed over the two pounds. It was too late. She picked up the box.

As she raced down the stairs, hugging the big box as if she somehow wished she could hide it inside her body, she began to feel giddy. The lights on Nelson's Christmas tree began to blur into each other and the sound of the carols over the speakers became echoey and distorted. Daniel would be so angry. And who could blame him? Her heart was racing. She put the GI Action Gun box down by her feet and leant against the perfume counter.

"Are you okay, Miss?"

It was an assistant. Miriam smiled and nodded but it can't have been too convincing because the assistant nodded back uncertainly. The last thing Miriam wanted was any kind of fuss so she bent down to pick up the GI Action Gun but she knocked the box against the counter and, wedged there momentarily, the sharp cardboard corner dug into her ankle. The pain was intense and she wanted to scream out in agony but the young assistant had already gone across to her supervisor and now both of them were looking over at her. Miriam picked up the box and walked out of the shop, desperately trying not to limp or cry. The pain from her ankle was unlike any pain she had ever felt before. She looked down. At least there was no blood.

FORTY SIX

"And you say that you knocked it?"

"I feel so stupid. It's probably nothing."

Dr Rahmanzai prodded the white bulge on Miriam's ankle with his thumb.

"Feel anything?"

Miriam shook her head.

"It used to hurt there. That's where I hit it in the first place. But now it's moved up here. To my knee."

"Let's take a look."

As the doctor fiddled in his drawer for something Miriam looked around the consulting room. It was the first time she had been in Bethel's new, purpose-built surgery. The last time she had been to see the doctor had been about the stupid poisoning. Back then the surgery had been little more than a converted back room in the village hall. This was different. There was a proper desk and there was even a couch on the other side of the room with some screens in case they were needed. On the wall there was a poster of a man who had had one half of his body skinned so that his muscles and inner organs were plainly visible. That must have frightened the children she thought.

"When did you hit your ankle Mrs Meredith?"

"Almost two weeks ago."

"And in that time the pain has gone and now it's in your knee?"

Miriam nodded. She didn't like the look on the doctor's face.

"Is it serious or anything?"

Dr Rahmanzai wrote something down on a piece of paper before ripping it out matter-of-factly and handing it to her.

"A course of mild painkillers," he said. "Take two of them every four hours or so after food and that should clear it up. I would recommend that you take regular exercise Mrs Meredith. Walk as much as you can so that the knee receives regular traction. With a bit of luck it should all be back to normal in plenty of time for Christmas."

She didn't want to ruin Christmas but hiding the limp from Daniel and the boy was difficult, as was resisting the constant urge to wince and cry out in pain. Only when Daniel had left for work and the boy had been packed off to school would she flop onto the sofa and cry. She took the pills as directed by Dr Rahmanzai but now, after three days, the pain was not getting any better. If anything it was more intense. She wondered if she should go back and ask for something stronger. She walked too, just like he'd advised her to – or at least she tried to. Every time she put pressure on her left foot the pain in her knee was like someone pushing a knife into it and twisting it. That was why she tried to time her walks so that there would be fewer people around. Putting on her thick raincoat she would go down the remote public footpath towards Tyddyn Andrew Farm but, every day, the distance covered would become shorter and shorter before the pain took over. She would sometimes sit down on the wet grass among the nettles and thistles, rocking herself as she cried.

Caernarfon was all wrong. The street was at an angle and the shops weren't straight. People were coming up to her but she couldn't understand what they were saying. It sounded as if they were hundreds of feet away and talking underwater. Carols in the background sounded like bells becoming ever higher and higher in pitch until, eventually, they tinkled. One woman's face in a headscarf was closer than all the others and she kept saying the same words over and over again but she couldn't understand them. Her chest felt as small and as tight as a walnut. It needed more air but she couldn't provide it. The pain was too intense. The street came up to meet her. Punched her hard on her cheek with its tarmac. The woman in the headscarf started screaming. Closing her eyes Miriam heard the tinkling. She saw the ballerina in the box once again – spinning, then fading. Vanishing into blackness.

FORTY SEVEN

How could there be so many doctors and nurses going by and yet none of them had anything to say about Miriam? Surely one of them must know something? Just a scrap of information would have been enough. A word to say that she was alright. But Daniel had given up asking. The last nurse he'd stopped had smiled sweetly but told him that someone was sure to be along in a while but nobody had. Doctors swept by with white coats flapping like the wings of seagulls. Phones. Ringing constantly. The sound of trolleys and lifts pinging open and shut. The smell of disinfectant.

Daniel stood up and walked down the corridor towards the coffee machine for the third time in an hour. He didn't need a coffee. In fact it was terrible coffee. But there was something reassuringly normal in slipping one of those new decimal coins into the slot, watching the plastic cup drop down and listening as the coffee thundered in with the force of horse piss. At least the alcove where the coffee machine had been placed was a change of scenery. Someone had tried to spruce it up with some trimmings and a fat, uncaring Santa but Christmas, even though it was only two weeks away, felt unreal. Like something that couldn't really happen now. Something that should be cancelled. Everyone would surely understand.

There was a row of red plastic chairs and on one there was a miserable-looking woman who was dabbing her face with a handkerchief. Next to her sat a man who Daniel assumed to be her husband. The man was holding the woman's hand and looking helpless, almost stunned. Catching his eye unexpectedly, Daniel pursed his lips into a sympathetic expression and the man nodded back his appreciation. There were little tragedies all around him and yet people somehow coped. They weren't screaming or climbing the walls. Perhaps that came later. After the waiting.

In the corner there was a man in a wheelchair who was staring intently at Daniel and he felt unnerved. He had visited Liverpool's Broadgreen Hospital every single night for the past week and he knew that it attracted a lot of strange people, so Daniel took his coffee and was about to walk back to his regular spot when the man in the wheelchair rolled out and blocked his path.

"You wouldn't go by without saying hello would you?"

It was a London accent. Daniel opened his mouth in preparation to say something well-meaning and polite but, as he did so, he looked into the man's face and noticed that there was something familiar about it. The stranger in the wheelchair cackled giving a brief glimpse of a largely toothless mouth.

"Don't remember me do you?"

"No, I'm afraid I..."

"Sit down."

The man in the wheelchair patted the vacant plastic chair beside him invitingly. He smelled vaguely of tobacco and stale whiskey but he seemed sober.

"I can't stay long," said Daniel, peeking nervously up the corridor. "One of the doctors might come looking for me. It's my wife."

"They'll find you," said the stranger. He patted the vacant chair again. "Come on. Sit down. There's a lot to be said for sitting. I do it all day long."

Daniel glanced up the corridor again but all he saw were more nurses rushing past the chair he'd been perched on for the past couple of hours without even bothering to check if he was still there. Broadgreen Hospital was like an enormous machine and it ran just as effectively if he was there or not. He would get his turn with the doctor eventually. Everybody did. He sat down on the plastic chair.

"You know," said the stranger. "I often wondered about you."

Daniel began to wonder if sitting down had been a mistake. The man was clearly a bit mad.

"Oh?"

The man in the wheelchair smiled to himself and shook his head as if he was watching something only he could see.

"I could tell straight away. I'd seen a lot of them come and go. But you could always tell the ones that were going somewhere."

He broke away from his reverie, sat forward in his chair, dropped his voice and looked directly at Daniel.

"I wasn't the only one mind. The others could see it too. But they played a cunning game. Kept their cards close to their chest." He glanced over his shoulder as if he was imparting a great secret. "Keep 'em keen. That's the way they did things back then. Probably still do for all I know. I haven't been involved in it for a while. Well..." He smiled and tapped his missing legs. "How could I? Losing one was bad enough. When I lost the other I was about as much use as a castrated stud."

"*Hoppy?*"

The man in the wheelchair smiled back and it suddenly made sense. Even with the missing teeth and the fuller face, the Londoner from Daniel's previous life was unmistakable.

"Large as life Danny boy!"

Daniel placed the coffee cup down and hugged his old friend. As he did so he was surprised to find that he was crying.

"Hey," said Hoppy, pushing him away affectionately. "What's

the matter with you?"

Daniel sat up. He patted his pockets for a handkerchief or tissue but he couldn't find anything. Hoppy produced one.

"Go on. Take it. I gave up crying years ago mate. Who is it? Wife you say?"

Daniel nodded.

"Miriam."

"Got a photo?"

Daniel reached into his wallet and took out a creased square. He flattened it as best he could and handed it to Hoppy.

"Not a great one I'm afraid," he said. "It was taken a few years ago when we went with the boy to St Ives."

Hoppy studied the photo for a few seconds, nodded and handed it back.

"A boy?"

"Nine now."

"Chip off the old block?"

"Not quite. He tries. We have a kickabout in the garden but he's a bit slow and heavy. Moans when I kick one past him."

Hoppy smiled.

"Talent skips a generation so they say. Maybe there'll be a grandson."

"What about you? Any children?"

"One," said Hoppy. "Kenny. Joined the Merchant Navy as soon as he could. Desperate to get away. Comes back three or four times a year. Luckily I can remember what he looks like from the photographs. Got a granddaughter too. 'Grandad on Wheels' she calls me. Not quite strong enough to push me yet, but give her time. She keeps asking me if I'm going to grow another pair of legs. I tell her none of the leg seeds have worked in the greenhouse yet."

Daniel smiled. He nodded towards the second missing leg.
"What happened?"

Hoppy took a deep breath and sat back in his wheelchair.

"Long story. After Preston I left football and went to Africa. One night I was chased by a huge lion and he got me – not difficult catching a one-legged man, he had a three-leg advantage. Anyway, he dragged me back to his den and he and his mates put their bibs on, arranged some candles and cutlery and they suppered on my leg until there was nothing left except gristle and bone. It took the hyenas to finish those bits off."

Daniel smiled cynically.

"Still the joker."

Hoppy sat forward again.

"Broke it in a fall if you must know. Usual tale. Got infected. Gangrene set in and the doctors said it had to come off. Buggered my chances with the Olympic relay team."

Hoppy had expected his old friend to laugh but Daniel just sipped his coffee.

"Miriam might lose hers."

He finished his coffee, scrunched up the plastic cup and threw it into the bin. The elderly couple stared at him disapprovingly.

"And it's all my stupid fault. She hit her leg."

"Wasn't your fault then was it? Could have happened to anyone."

"I know. But then she said it kept hurting and I just told her to take an aspirin. I was so selfish. She started moaning about her knee and I was in the middle of something so I just snapped at her and told her to go to the bloody doctor if it was bothering her that much. I was wrapped in my poetry and my own daft ambitions. Trying to win the chair at the National and be a great bard." He shook his head and laughed sardonically. "Is it any wonder that, in the old days, some poets were also called fools?"

Two young nurses scurried past towards some distant emergency. There was a muffled announcement on the tannoy system that nobody took any notice of.

"Still writing then?"

Daniel nodded. He sighed and studied his feet.

"Goalkeepers and poets," said Hoppy. "They're a breed apart. Never could understand either of them if I'm honest."

He smiled. Daniel looked up at him and smiled back.

A doctor walked towards them and stopped. He was looking at Daniel.

"Mr Meredith? Can you come with me please?"

FORTY EIGHT

The side room was small and smelled of pine disinfectant. Nobody had bothered to put up any tinsel.

"My name is Doctor Kennedy, I believe up to now you've dealt with Doctor Quinn but it's been transferred over to my department now and – sit down Mr Meredith, let me move those papers for you."

Daniel waited until the doctor had shifted a pile of magazines before he sat down on a red plastic chair identical to the ones in the corridor.

"We're in the process of re-developing the department," said Dr Kennedy, sitting behind the desk and laying down his medical notes like a pianist with his score. "Normally we'd have a quieter space but, for now, we have to grab any room we can I'm afraid. Sorry about that. Now..." he flicked through the medical notes and whipped on a pair of thick, horn-rimmed glasses. He studied the notes for a few seconds, made a grunting noise, checked something on another piece of paper before finally taking off his glasses and placing his elbows on the table like a bank manager.

"It's a procedure we've carried out before," he said. "But that doesn't mean to say that it's straightforward or without risks."

"Is she going to lose her leg?"

Dr Kennedy opened his mouth to say something but thought better of it. He put on his glasses and checked his notes, running his finger down one of the papers until he found what he was looking for. He looked up.

"It says here you have a son?"

"Nine years old. Yes. He's with his grandparents while I'm staying in Liverpool."

"And you're staying in?"

"The Rocket. It's a pub. Just round the corner."

"Yes, I know it."

Daniel was getting impatient with such trifling details. Why did he need to know these things?

"Is she going to lose her leg?"

Dr Kennedy sighed.

"It's a difficult time, Mr Meredith."

Daniel pushed back the chair, stood up and turned to face the wall as if he was daring it to a fight.

"*Jesus!*"

"Try to remain calm."

Daniel turned round, his rage a rabid dog on a leash.

"You ask me if I have a son. Do *you* have a son doctor? Do *you* have to try to sound cheerful on the phone every night to him? Pretending that everything is going to be okay and that his Mum is going to come home soon and that life will carry on as normal? What happens when Santa doesn't bring all the presents he wanted? What happens when Christmas doesn't come?"

"Please," said Doctor Kennedy, extending his hand in the direction of the pushed back plastic chair. "Sit down Mr Meredith."

Daniel knew he was powerless and he felt stupid for having lost his temper. He sighed and sat down again.

"I'm sorry, doctor."

"She'll be going into surgery tomorrow morning. I notice here that the surgeon is Mr Blandford, one of our most experienced and skillful men so she'll be in capable hands. But I should also point out to you that this isn't a procedure that's entirely without risk."

Daniel felt all the saliva draining from his mouth.

"So she's going to lose her leg?"

"It's..."

The pause lasted a hundred years. Somewhere from outside there were carol singers. It sounded as if it was coming from a distant galaxy. The world had gone mad. Christmas made no sense. Nothing made sense.

"It's *what? Tell me* for fuck's sake!"

Dr Kennedy looked up. Daniel couldn't see his eyes because of the glare of the lights on the glasses. He suddenly looked like some sort of alien. Not a human being at all.

"When Mrs Meredith knocked her leg it caused a blood clot. Now normally these things are pretty straightforward and they can be dealt with reasonably quickly but this went undetected for long enough for it to prove problematic."

"*Problematic.* What does that mean?"

"What that means Mr Meredith is that the clot travelled up through your wife's body. First it reached the knee – which is why she suffered those excruciating pains whenever she put pressure on it."

"But the doctor told her to ignore it and keep walking! That's what he said! He gave her some pills and said that it would go away!"

"Sadly it was a misdiagnosis. Rare. But they do happen unfortunately."

"So it was his fault!"

"It's nobody's fault Mr Meredith."

"How can you sit there and say that? A doctor says don't worry about it and to take a bloody aspirin and now she's on her way to an operating theatre and she's going to lose a leg!"

Dr Kennedy took off his glasses and placed them carefully on top of the medical notes. He leant forward, his hands clenched together. Daniel noticed that his knuckles were very white.

"I'm afraid it might be more serious than that. You see, the clot has moved up to her left lung and..."

Dr Kennedy left the sentence hanging in the air like a black cloud. In the pause that followed Daniel heard the carol singers again. Another life. Trouble free. Christmas on the way.

"Can anything be done?"

"She's in the best possible hands."

"But she's not going to die is she?"

"Get some rest Mr Meredith."

Daniel nodded like a man in a dream. He stood up. Leant against the wall for a second. Ran his hand through his hair. Then, as an afterthought, he turned back.

"Sorry for... you know... shouting..."

Doctor Kennedy smiled a smile that wasn't a smile.

Daniel staggered back to the coffee machine like a man walking away from a plane crash. Nurses and patients bumped into him but he hardly registered the impact. Hoppy was gone. In his place was a young mother and two children. She was searching frantically through her purse for some coins. Seeing Daniel she looked up. Her face was lined and her mascara was running.

"You haven't got any change have you love? For the machine."

Daniel stared at her for a moment as if she was speaking a foreign language. Then, slowly, her words fell into place and he searched his pocket. It was full of coppers. He gave them all to the woman.

He walked back towards The Rocket. Behind him, the seemingly endless sprawl of Broadgreen Hospital lay like a stranded spaceship. Miriam was in there somewhere. Unreachable. There was nothing he could do. One small life that made sense of his entire world and he'd been too selfish to see it. He carried on walking along the path to the zebra crossing. There was a newsagent's across the road. He took out his wallet and peeled out a pound note to buy a pack of Woodbines and a box of matches.

Back in his room in The Rocket he shut himself off as much as he could from the noise of the bar downstairs. He lit a Woodbine and the smoke felt divine. He finished it, lit another, placed it in the ashtray and took out his notebook from the desk drawer. He clicked his pen and wrote until The Rocket was quiet and until only one or two cars whooshed by in the street below. After that he was alone in the world and he wrote of love and death and loss, of fear and shame and regret. All of it in his neatest hand. All of it effortless. All of it in perfect cynghanedd.

FORTY NINE

They were coming for him. Hundreds of them. Possibly thousands. He wasn't going to lie there and count. All he could see were their eyes in the dark – cold jewel eyes glinting as they caught the moon. Now they were crawling all over him. Their legs pushing into his body. Prodding. Kneading. And the noise. The constant howling and mewling. On his face. The warm fur. The needle claws on his cheeks. The razor teeth cutting into his skin. Their tiny faces signifying evil. Still they came. Pouring in through the door like a burst riverbank. He took their lives. Now they would take his.

The Hangman shot up in bed. It took him a good few seconds to realise that the bedroom was empty. Beside him, Leah was snoring gently. Apart from that the only sound was the occasional rush of a breeze outside and the bored clipping of the clock.

He was wet. He checked to see if he'd pissed himself but he quickly realised it was just sweat and the nightmare came back to him. Hundreds and thousands of crazed kittens tumbling into the room and jumping on the bed. But there were no kittens now. It was safe.

Pushing back the bedclothes he stood up, unhooked the dressing gown from behind the door, stepped into his slippers and went downstairs.

The lights had been left on the Christmas tree in the lounge. He switched them off. He went into the kitchen and opened the back door. The air was freezing and he shivered. He grabbed the keys to the shed.

The door creaked open and The Hangman walked up to the big wooden barrel. Removing the lid he gazed in at the still, black water. How many bags had he plunged into it over the years? Holding them down until the writhing and the muted mewling stopped? Tiny lives without testament or record. Innocent lives. Denied a grave.

The Hangman tipped the heavy barrel until the icy water engulfed his feet, ankles and splashed up to his knees – cold, sharp, intense and cleansing. Resisting the urge to step away he held on with all his strength until the barrel was empty. Only then did he roll it back and replace the lid.

He locked the shed door and stood with his sodden dressing gown as tight as a second skin. The grass and the mud around his slippers sizzled. He looked up. The moon and the stars were silent witnesses to his baptism.

FIFTY

Someone had plucked her from her old world. Not that she was complaining. The old world had been one of pain. When she closed her eyes in this one it felt as if she was on a warm beach, lying down with the waves whispering in the distance and the trees above her head rustling a lullaby. It was an island. She was pretty sure of that. Far away from everywhere. Sometimes there were voices. They always spoke quietly and the language was unfamiliar. They were speaking quietly so as not to disturb her, she knew that. She was a visitor from the other side of the world who had been washed up unexpectedly on their shores so it was natural that they should be a little bit wary but she would sometimes stretch out her arm to try to tell them it was fine and that they could come over and talk to her if they wanted. But they only came close when it was time for some food and drink. They would leave it on a tray in front of her and then move away, silent as little puffs of smoke. After the food they would give her a special drink and then, slowly, the island would turn into night and she felt it falling away from her like a rock tumbling through black space.

The man who came to see her every day was familiar but she couldn't understand his words either. They sounded echoey, like he was talking from the back of a deep cave. He would hold her hand and stroke it. It felt pleasant but she never spoke back although she did try to smile and, when she did, he smiled too, rubbing the back of her hand and speaking his unintelligible words. Usually the native girls would take him away after a while. He never wanted to let go of her hand but the girls gently unclasped it and he was gone. She wondered whether he was an important dignitary on the island. A priest perhaps. Or a chief.

One day she woke up to find that her bed was moving. She was still warm but, above her head, there were bright planets flitting past. The girls were by her side but there was also a man in a mask pushing her bed along a tunnel. They entered a place which she guessed must have been right at the centre of the island because it was full of natives rushing around and looking down at her. She didn't recognise any of the faces. They all wore masks. They tried to talk to her but nothing made sense. She tried to get up but one of the natives in masks held her down and placed something on her mouth. She breathed in. She wanted to rub her eyes but her arms were like lead. The man in the mask was looking down at her and talking. It sounded as if he was counting but she couldn't understand the numbers. The room became darker and she realised that she was dying. She closed her eyes and waited. It didn't hurt at all.

FIFTY ONE

The coffin was smaller than I'd expected. I couldn't imagine how they'd managed to fit the body in there without an element of force. The pall-bearers carried it along the narrow path of Llanddeiniolen cemetery, carefully avoiding the rocks and snake-like roots that lay like traps at unpredictable intervals. All it would take was one small mis-step and the coffin would crash down and the body would spill out of its silk cocoon. People would scream and I would have had to do something. Although I had no idea what.

As the coffin was slowly lowered into the hole I tried not to think of how the body would decompose over the next few months into a grimacing skeleton. I clung on to the face I had seen before the undertaker had put the lid in place. I had felt the hand and it had been icy. Those hands. Always so safe. Warm and protective, stroking me after a fall. Teaching me to tie my shoelaces. Ruffling my hair.

The vicar closed his Bible and the dirt was thrown down on top of the coffin. I wasn't sure if this was the end of the ceremony. I looked around cautiously. The vicar nodded at me and everyone moved away from the grave slowly and respectfully. Death was so incongruous on such a beautiful summer's day. The air was thick with buzzing wasps and wild, flapping butterflies. Fat bees, tripped out on pollen, lumbered from one flower to another and invisible birds gave the illusion that the trees themselves were singing. In the distance there was a purple glow over the tops of the houses in Bethel. Mount Orwig and Snowdon continued their ancient private battle, straining their peaks as high as they could towards the cloudless sky.

A line of people shook my hand and expressed their sympathy while I pulled appropriate faces and muttered 'thank yous.' There had been so many people. I had no idea who most of them were. The vicar was the last one. He said it was a great loss. I thanked him. He nodded again and walked away. I was left behind by the open grave.

"Do you mind if I..."

A bearded man in a denim jacket stepped forward. He was carrying a shovel.

"No," I said, understanding. "Go ahead."

"Thanks mate. It's just that we've got another one at three."

He began filling in the grave whilst cheerfully whistling the riff from *Purple Haze*.

As I left the cemetery I was distracted by a faint chirping sound to my right and, turning round, I noticed that a sudden light breeze had caught the blades of a cheerfully-coloured child's windmill. It had been stuck into the ground on top of a tiny grave which was also covered in cheap sweets – pick 'n' mix chews, jellies, string necklaces and the aniseed circles from liquorice allsorts. There were some bunches of wild flowers which had seen better days. This was the grave of the mysterious little girl. A sudden voice behind me made me jump.

"Come on, the car is waiting. We'll be late."

I turned and followed Miriam out of the cemetery.

FIFTY TWO

Bryn Hyfryd had been created by Sir Prydderch Collinge, a local architect made good. Being a typical architect, he had got bored with his project as soon as he'd finished designing it so, by the time he and his family had moved in, he had already begun dreaming up his next house. Architects were like chess players. Always two or three moves ahead.

Miriam handed Daniel the printed description sheets from Harris & Furlong Estate Agents of Caernarfon.

"It's too big," he said. "What do we need four bedrooms for? The boy will be off to college in a couple of years. We'll be rattling round that place like two marbles!"

"You could convert one of the spare bedrooms into an office."

"I've got an office. Out in the shed."

"But you're always saying how damp it is and that it's ruining your books."

"We can't afford it."

"Sam Furlong says the view is superb."

Daniel handed back the sheets.

"We can't afford it."

Miriam leant forward and ignored the offered sheets. She laid her hand on his. Daniel shifted defensively in his chair. Whenever Miriam adopted this pose he knew that she wasn't going to give up.

"You're a headmaster now."

"So?"

"And a chaired bard at the National Eisteddfod."

She nodded in the direction of the ornate wooden throne which had occupied the corner of the lounge for the past three years.

"There's no money in poetry, you know that."

Miriam tightened her grip on his hand.

"When those journalists came last month didn't you notice how they turned their noses up?"

"It's all in your mind."

"You saw it as clearly as I did. They seemed surprised that a bard lived in such a cramped house. And when you showed them that shabby writing shed, they couldn't believe it."

"Nonsense."

Daniel stood up. Went over to the window. Miriam followed him.

"The village isn't what it was. You've said so yourself. That youth club across the road at the village hall drives you bonkers. Then there are all the cars from the new estate. No one knows anyone anymore. When I go to the shop I don't recognise anyone. No one says hello."

The youth club did drive him mad. That was true.

"We can have a look I suppose," said Daniel. "No harm in that."

"Good. I'll give Harris and Furlong a ring."

FIFTY THREE

"An honour to meet you," said Mr Furlong, stepping out of his Vauxhall Viva and hurriedly stubbing out a cigarette with his heel. He extended his hand. "It's not every day I get to shake hands with a famous poet."

He was a thin man with greased-back hair and a pencil moustache.

"Lovely property," he said, immediately turning his attention to Miriam and guessing that she was the soft target. "Architect designed and built. Not many of those round here. Come and have a look inside. You'll be amazed."

He jangled the keys, fiddled them into the lock and ushered them into the hallway.

"It was built three years ago," he said, his voice echoing back from the bare walls. "Designed and built by Sir Prydderch Collinge. Do you know him?"

"Only to say hello," said Daniel.

"Lovely gentleman."

"Why is he selling?"

"Architects, Mr Meredith. You know what they're like."

He winked at Miriam as if she was in on some private game but when she didn't smile back he appeared to be slightly unnerved. But he picked himself up immediately.

"Sir Prydderch has just finished a new place on Anglesey for him and his family. Seven bedrooms. Right on the shore of the Menai Straits. Very nice. Anyway, this is the hall as you can see.

Very spacious. Very light."

"Those stairs look a bit dangerous," said Daniel. "They're just planks of wood stuck to the wall. There's no bannister or handrail or anything."

Mr Furlong smiled.

"Swedish Mr Meredith. All the rage apparently. That's what Sir Prydderch told me. Let me show you the kitchen."

Bryn Hyfryd's kitchen was a plain cage of wood and stainless steel.

"Where *is* everything?"

"It's a revolutionary new design concept, Mr Meredith. Sir Prydderch is a huge fan of Japanese houses and also of what he referred to as the Scandinavian minimalist approach."

It sounded like a line he'd practised rather too well in the car during his journey from Caernarfon. As soon as he'd delivered it he looked a little embarrassed. He cleared his throat.

"It's all here though. Dishwasher, washing machine, dryer, fridge – one of those snazzy American ones in fact – all included in the price. Let me show you the lounge."

It was like walking into a barn. Shorn of all furniture and completely carpetless their footsteps and voices bounced off the white-painted walls like ball-bearings.

"Very spacious as you can see. Lots of possibilities here. Look on it as a blank canvas."

Daniel looked across the cavernous room towards the cinemascopic window.

"Why are those curtains drawn?"

"Ah," said Mr Furlong. "The *pièce de la résistance* as they say. Let me show you."

The estate agent strode across the stripped floorboards and pulled a cord. When the curtains separated to reveal the view it was such a spectacular revelation that Daniel half expected it to be accompanied by a choir of angels. He stepped forward as if in a daze.

"The view is quite something isn't it, Mr Meredith?"

The double windows presented a glorious still of Snowdon on a clear day, its jagged incisor jabbing a blue sky. The only movement was a puff of smoke indicating that the tourist train to the summit was about halfway up.

"What's the asking price again?"

"We've got it on the market for twenty seven and a half."

Daniel gazed out at Snowdon. He took a sharp intake of breath and shook his head dismissively.

"Far too expensive."

Two months later we moved in.

FIFTY FOUR

"How did you find me?"

"I'm good at tracking. You should know that by now. And this is such a big house. My place is tiny. I can just about fit Arrluk in beside me. You wouldn't know Arrluk. He's my best husky. He wanted to come tonight but I needed him to stay behind to protect the fish."

"I never thought I'd see you again."

"You don't need me anymore. That's fine. It's nothing to be sad about."

"I almost wish I was a kid and could be scared of the curtains and the damson tree again."

"So, your Mum almost died."

"That was a long time back. No one told me very much though. They just said there was something wrong with her leg. I had no idea at the time. I suppose they wanted to protect me."

"I did call. But you weren't there."

"Dad sent me to live with my Pantglyn Nain and Taid for a bit while he stayed in Liverpool near the hospital. Mum's okay now. They saved her. She cried when she came home though. I couldn't really understand why. I thought she'd have been happy."

"So now your Dad's famous?"

"Yeah, kind of. People stop him in the street in Caernarfon or Bangor and they want to shake his hand but it's no big deal. Mum loves it. Thinks she's the Queen of Wales!"

"My Dad was famous too."

"You never said. What was he famous for?"

"For being big. He was the biggest eskimo in the North Pole. His name was Siluk and he was eight feet tall. Some say he was even taller but people like to make stuff up. I do remember that all the children in the village would shelter behind him in the storms though. The mad winter storms turned the snow into white whips and when they lashed against your face you felt it. You could even feel those lashes when you were wrapped up in your skins and coats. So all the children in our village would huddle behind Siluk as they moved into a larger hut where the fires were. It was said that Siluk was so wide that even when the children formed a circle they still couldn't wrap their arms around him. Siluk was a hero to everyone but I was also scared of him because his face was so difficult to see behind his fur hood and his beard. I couldn't see if he was pleased or angry with me. I can't ever remember him smiling. I suppose it wasn't the kind of place where people smiled a lot. Still isn't."

"Why do you stay?"

"Where else can I go?"

"New York. London. All those fantastic places."

"Don't think so. I'm happy with Arrluk. Yesterday we tracked a bear for three miles. He was such a beautiful creature. But the world is melting. Everywhere's getting smaller. When me and Arrluk walk the ice we can hear it crack under our feet. It used to be thick as a mountain."

"Well I'm not staying. I'm fed up with this dump."

"But it's so beautiful."

"Everyone says that. But they're just the people who visit. Pity us the poor sods who have to live here all year. No bands ever come. You have to wait six weeks for new films to come to the Majestic. This world's melting and getting smaller too. But I'm not going down with it."

"Won't you miss your friends? What was that guy's name?

"Llew. He's got new friends now. We lost touch when I stayed on at school. He said he wanted money so he got a job, an apprenticeship in a garage. He loves all that."

"Where will you go?"

"As far away from here as possible."

"I'd better go. Arrluk will be waiting."

"Will I see you again?"

"Maybe."

"Miko, wait."

"What?"

"I just wanted to say, you know, thanks. Thanks for being there. For looking after me when I was young and when I was afraid of the damson tree."

"Hope you get where you want to go. Goodbye."

FIFTY FIVE

The sea despised Llandudno's concrete promenade but however hard it thrashed and crashed there was no way it could bash it down. Not that it showed any sign of giving up. With a groan, Daniel leant forward in the front seat of my BMW.

"I can't hear it."

"It's okay. Sit back. I'll do it."

I turned up the volume on the DAB radio.

"– nchester United three... Wolverhampton Wanders one... Everton nil... Arsenal nil... Burnley two... Chelse –"

"She's late."

"She's always late Dad. You know what she's like when she goes shopping."

"Spending money like there's no tomorrow."

"– ston Villa nil... Fulham nil... Manchester City one... Leeds United two... Liverpool two... Sunderla –"

"Switch it off."

"But they haven't finished yet."

"I want to hear the wind. And put the wipers on. So we can look down on the beach. I like beaches in winter."

I killed the radio and turned the ignition in order to put on the wipers. They sliced the rain like swords.

"Don't leave them on too long though. They drain the battery."

"I know Dad."

We sat in silence for a minute or so listening to the intermittent hum of the wipers, the gravel-like strikes of the rain and the desperation of the wind.

"You should look after your mother."

"What do you mean?"

I knew what he meant.

"You should come home more often. London is so far away."

"We've been through this Dad. I come back when I can. But it's not always easy."

"Can't imagine why you couldn't get a job closer to home."

"Dad, London *is* my home now."

The beach was grey and deserted. Seagulls hung in the air like handkerchiefs on invisible sticks. The sea was the colour of iron.

"I'm eighty two now. And your mother's getting on too."

"She's as strong as an ox. And so are you."

He grunted and faced the beach again.

"How can anyone live in London?"

"It's just like a series of small towns."

"No one knows anybody."

"I've got friends. It's really no different to anywhere else."

He grunted again.

"And divorced too."

"We've been through this."

"After only three years of marriage. Three years is nothing."

I turned to him and tried not to lose my calm.

"Dad, it didn't work out. Me and Maxine tried but in the end it was for the best. We still get on. It was all very amicable."

"At least there were no children I suppose. That's something to be grateful for. And I bet even if there had been you wouldn't have sent them to a Welsh school would you? There are plenty of them in London you know."

I was back because he was dying. I wondered if he knew. Miriam had called me three days earlier and she had broken down on the phone. The doctors had given him less than three months. Cancer spreading like a stain.

"You've put on weight."

"Sitting down all day Dad. I try to work some of it off in the gym but it never goes away."

"You were always slow."

Miriam was always on the verge of tears and it was impossible to know if Daniel noticed. His eyes were always focussed on something on a distant horizon. When he watched the television he appeared to be seeing through it. They were the eyes of a man who had travelled to the end of the earth and who wasn't sure if he wanted to come back. Food didn't work. He ate a few mouthfuls and then pushed his plate away. Miriam tried showing him old photographs to rekindle his interest in life but, even though he played along and put on his glasses, he simply nodded and his attention drifted after two or three snaps. He claimed he couldn't remember who anybody was.

A couple of nights after I'd arrived from London I had suggested we both pop out into the back garden for a little kickabout like we used to in the old house. Nothing too strenuous, just for fun. It was a relatively calm evening and, although the grass looked a little bit soggy and overgrown I reckoned that it might be okay for a slow half hour or so whilst Miriam could cry without being seen or heard.

He stood there, arms hanging loosely by his sides in classic goalkeeper pose – spitting on his hands and rubbing them together – urging me to give it all I had. I made a good show of pretending to think about where I was going to kick it but, in the end, I tapped it at medium pace to his left so that it was an easy stop for him with his foot. He laughed as he bent down slowly to pick up the ball. Throwing it back with contempt he told me that I would have to try harder than that so, when it came to the next kick, I tapped it slightly harder, this time to his right – but I made sure that he could stop this one too without having to dive. In the old days I would never have got one past him. Now I could easily have scored all day. The longer we stayed out the louder his wheezing became. It was as if there was too much air still left in the world. He was getting tired of having to breathe it all in.

The rain splashed like a cascade of tiny pebbles across the BMW's windscreen.

"She'll have bought a new dress," said Daniel. "She always does. Of course she'll try to hide it in a bunch of other bags and hope I won't notice. I always do though. Not that I mind anymore. But it's nice that she thinks I do."

He half-turned to me and smiled. It was the smile that shocked me when I'd arrived from London a week earlier. Miriam had rushed out of Bryn Hyfryd's front door to hug me as soon as I was out of the car – crying uncontrollably and trying not to let Daniel see. When I'd seen him standing in the doorway his smile had the effect of stretching the skin on his face almost to ripping point. The shape of his skull was now shockingly apparent beneath the wisps of white hair; hair which had once been so black and luxuriant. He was deteriorating before our very eyes, like a stop-motion film. I shook his hand and felt his bones. His head didn't have enough skin. His mouth was too big for his face.

"Will you ever move back?"

"Maybe."

"We miss you son."

"Dad, I do what I can. It's been a difficult time. I phone every night. I come home whenever I get the chance. But it's tricky."

"I know."

He was looking away. Out through the side window at nothing in particular. After sighing heavily he stared straight ahead at the empty beach with the handkerchief seagulls. The scene was replenished every few seconds by the windscreen wipers. The wind was so strong now it rocked the BMW like a gang of unseen rioters.

"Someone should go and collect her," he said.

"Who?"

"The little girl."

He nodded in the direction of the beach but all I could see were fierce waves smashing onto sand and shingle.

"What girl?"

He turned to me as if I was playing some kind of joke on him.

"Down there," he said, gesturing towards the waves. "With the plastic windmill and the bags of sweets. She must belong to someone. She's been there for a while. Poor thing. Must be freezing."

Two weeks later he was gone.

FIFTY SIX

Miriam sat by the window in her reclining chair staring out at Snowdon, the coffee undrunk on her little table, long gone cold. Whenever I turned to my book she would sigh and I felt guilty so I folded the corner of the page, put it down and stared at Snowdon too even though it was smothered in cloud. UK Gold murmured unobtrusively on the big TV. They'd bought it from Dixons in Bangor five or six years earlier, primarily for the football on Sky Sports. The salesman, straight from school, had given Daniel his well-practised spiel about it being HD-ready and loaded with options for 5.1 Dolby Digital stereo but Daniel had just nodded patiently as if he was dealing with a slightly annoying foreigner and, as soon as he'd finished his performance, he'd said he'd take it providing there was a discount for cash.

'HD ready' was wasted on the blurred re-runs of *Last of the Summer Wine* and *Columbo* but Miriam didn't mind. She didn't care about clarity of sound or vision. What she liked was the familiarity and the comfort of Compo, Clegg and all the others. She had enjoyed watching them when Daniel had been alive and she enjoyed them now, although she did sometimes turn to her left to share a laugh only to remember that he wasn't there anymore. On the phone I had often suggested new things that she might like – recommendations from *The Observer* or *The Guardian* regarding new crime dramas on Channel 4 or the BBC which might challenge her a little but I soon discovered that she didn't want challenges. She wanted reassurance. Being challenged was fine if you were young, she insisted, but when you got older you just wanted to know that things were predictable and familiar. She insisted that one day I would understand. When *my* world had fallen apart.

"Did you hear the storm last night?"

"No," I said, turning away from the shrouded Snowdon and looking at her. She was still in her green dressing gown and slippers even though it was almost noon.

"I thought the roof was going to blow off."

"The roof won't blow off Mum. This house was built by an architect."

She sipped her coffee. When she realised it was cold she pulled a face and put it down again, wiping her mouth with some kitchen roll.

"Shall I make you another?

"No, I'm fine. It's almost lunchtime. I'll make some sandwiches in a minute."

"I can do it."

"I need to get dressed too."

Last of the Summer Wine came to an end. It was the third episode Miriam had watched that morning and there were eight more on the schedule. She pressed the 'off' button on her remote and the room was plunged into silence. We both looked at Snowdon. She sighed.

"So you think I'm making a big mistake don't you?"

"I didn't say that Mum. All I said is that it's up to you."

In the corner there was a shrine to Daniel's memory – one framed photograph of him in his National Eisteddfod chair and, beneath it, a vase of fresh flowers and a flickering candle. She lit it every morning and blew it out again at night. I had seen boxes of fresh candles in the cupboard.

"Moving house is not a mistake if that's what you really want to do Mum. I mean, this is a really big place for just one person so I can see the logic."

"He always said it was too big. If it wasn't for this view I don't think we'd have come."

I hated the house. Always had done. Pretentious and impractical it had been created for the eye rather than for the realities of life. The plank-like stairs would have looked great in an interiors magazine but for a woman in her mid-to-late seventies like Miriam they were a potential death-trap. She had slipped a couple of times on her way to bed – in the dark in order to save electricity (even though the ever-careful Daniel had left her enough to live out her days in considerable comfort) – I had insisted that she fit a stairlift. When she had protested I had even insisted on paying for it. Sir Prydderch Collinge may have coughed in his immaculately-brewed coffee had he seen how his minimalist vision had been desecrated by a Stannah but Sir Prydderch Collinge could go fuck himself. I doubted very much whether the likes of Sir Prydderch Collinge had ever had to listen to their elderly mothers crying on the phone in the small hours of the morning because they'd slipped on the stairs and chipped their collar-bone.

"I've seen a bungalow."

"Another one?"

"This time it's different."

"You always say that."

"Well if you don't want to listen you can go back to London and take your book with you."

She turned away like a sulky young girl and looked at the cloud where Snowdon used to be. I sighed.

"Where is this bungalow?"

"Llanrug."

"Mum, that's only down the road! What's the point? What's

Llanrug got that this place hasn't?"

"A shop for a start. The one here has closed. And the chapel has been turned into a carpet warehouse. Llanrug's got a lovely chapel."

"You don't know anyone in Llanrug."

"I can make friends."

"You're rubbish at making friends Mum."

She turned to me.

"What's it to you where I live anyway? You're down in London. I only ever see you when we go to St Ives and when you *want* something." She sipped her cold coffee and muttered under her breath. "Money usually."

"I'm here now and I don't want anything. I came to see you."

"Yes. Well."

Her 'yes well' was always a brick wall in any conversation. If there was anything that challenged her or spoiled her flow or which threatened to take the conversation into areas that she didn't want to follow she would say it and that would be that. Subject closed. And I would have to start again using a different tack.

"Where in Llanrug is it?"

"By the main road."

"It'll be noisy."

"Be nice to hear some life. The only thing I can hear from here is the wind when it's stormy. And I know it's going to blow the roof off one day. I don't care what you say about bloody architects. I'm the one who sleeps here all alone and I'm the one who can feel the foundations shaking. There's nothing between me and that mountain to soften the blow. I get the full force."

"Do you want me to come with you for a look?"

She put down the cup and changed her tone.

"Would you?"

"If you're serious about it yes."

"I am."

"Well, if you're sure."

"I've arranged to see it tomorrow at two. I've even started sorting out some of my things. The attic room is full of papers and books. Most of it needs throwing out. Daniel was such a hoarder. Lots of your old things up there too. I didn't know what you wanted keeping so I left out all the boxes."

"I'll go up and sort it this afternoon."

FIFTY SEVEN

One half of the attic room was completely blocked up by boxes, some wooden but mostly cardboard. The air was dry and dusty and it scraped the back of my throat making me cough. The floorboards creaked ominously beneath my feet as I walked across. The only light came from a tiny window which was greasy with grime and which probably hadn't been opened since Sir Prydderch Collinge's builders slotted it in. I felt as if I was standing in Tutankhamen's tomb.

Where to start? I sat down cross-legged like a boy scout and dragged over the first box. It was stuffed with stinky old curtains. Why would anyone want to keep old curtains? I pulled them out, unfurling them like a mad snake charmer until the dust made me sneeze and I was forced to unroll a piece of dried tissue paper from my pockets to blow my nose. There were some papers in the bottom of the box. Faded holiday brochures from the seventies. Special offers that had long since expired from travel companies which had gone to the wall or merged or been taken over. I imagined what would happen if I filled out one of the coupons asking for more information and posted it. Would it fall through the letterbox of a derelict building somewhere in the middle of Manchester or London? Or into a P.O. Box full of spiders?

Pushing the box aside I pulled forward another. Plastic coat hangers tangled up with an old belt. I pushed that aside too. The next box contained old photo albums. I slid one out and wiped the leather cover with the back of my sleeve. The long-shut album creaked as I opened it and a small square slid out on to the floor. I picked it up and turned it over. It was a small black and white print of me as a little boy, possibly aged six or seven, standing next to Gladys and Auntie Kate by the pond in Llys Meifor's garden. Both women were squinting into the camera because of the bright sunlight and my arm had been raised over my forehead so that the shadow obscured half my face.

Miriam's voice came from the landing.

"Are you alright up there? I'm just about to make some tea."

"I'm fine," I said, raising my voice a little. "Just making a start. I'll be down in a bit."

I heard her muttering as she padded across to the stairs down to the kitchen, having another of her one-sided conversations with Daniel.

I flicked hurriedly through the pages of the photo album – Daniel with a pair of binoculars leaning on the bonnet of the old Ford Popular, his hair black, thick and wavy. There was another of him in his Caernarfon Town goalie's shirt, smiling and holding a ball. He couldn't have been more than seventeen. I turned the page and saw Miriam, young and beautiful, standing in the middle of a country road wearing a white skirt which seemed almost luminous in the surrounding gloom. She had been caught in mid-laugh and it was an expression I had never seen from her before. An image of pure love. I was slightly puzzled. She'd always told me that she'd met Daniel when she was just short of twenty. Yet she looked much younger in the photograph.

I closed the album and stood up, being careful not to hit my head on the low beams, but as I turned to cross the floor towards the ladder I almost tripped over a pile of old shoeboxes bearing the name of a Mr Oliver and Sons, Caernarfon. One of them had been knocked over and it had spewed out a pile of yellowed letters tied together with elastic. I bent down and replaced them as best I could but the last of the letters was unopened. It had been addressed to Miriam at the old house.

I noticed that it had a Dublin postmark.

FIFTY EIGHT

Miriam didn't recognise him until it was too late. Struggling in the rain along Caernarfon's High Street towards the car park with her bag of shopping from Morrisons she had clocked the half-familiar face from a distance and he had obviously seen her too. Now she wished she had kept her head down. She wasn't in the mood for a conversation. Let alone with him.

"Let me help you with that," he said, trying to take the heavy bag.

"No, it's fine Cerwyn. I'm almost there."

"Almost *where* girl?"

"The car park. The new multi-storey. I've got a disabled badge so it's okay."

"Don't be daft. Let me buy you a coffee. I haven't seen you in ages."

Miriam flicked through a stream of possible excuses in her head but none of them sounded plausible enough to say out loud so, allowing him to take her bag she followed him into the new Costa Coffee bar and sat by the window.

"What will you have?"

Miriam took off her glasses, wiped the lens with her hankie and squinted to read the list of exotic coffees.

"Oh, I don't know. Anything. You choose. I can't stay long though."

"Americano?"

"Yes. Fine. Whatever."

But he didn't go immediately. He stared at her. Smiled.

"Good to see you, Miriam."

She smiled back. Then, to her relief, he unpeeled a tenner from his wallet and went off to queue up at the counter behind a woman holding her screaming toddler.

"I'm not sure if it was worth all the effort," he said.

"What?"

"Poetry. Did Daniel ever feel like that?"

"I don't know. He never said. I don't think so."

"No, well, maybe that was the difference between him and me. Between mediocrity and brilliance."

She felt momentarily sorry for him.

"You're too hard on yourself, Cerwyn. You always were."

He leant forwards, placing both elbows on the table. His expression was one of great seriousness.

"You know our problem in Wales? We never conquered anyone."

Miriam smiled, shook her head and sipped her coffee.

"I'm serious," said Cerwyn. "That was our big mistake. We sat here for centuries just twiddling our thumbs whilst the rest of the world trampled all over us, priding ourselves on surviving when, really, we should have gone on the land-grabbing rampage like everybody else. I used to hate the English but you know what? Now I admire them. Yes, I know. Me. The Hangman! Who'd have thought such a thing?"

He laughed. Miriam smiled. She blew on her Americano and wished it wasn't so hot.

"Colonization is an evil thing in so many ways but I tell you this Miriam, it's a brilliant way of extending your language and culture. And that's what the English did. They conquered the world. They gave it cricket, tea and Shakespeare. And what did we give the world? Absolutely nothing. Nobody reads our poetry unless it's in English. We talk to ourselves girl. Always have done. Swimming around in circles that get smaller and smaller every year. Seeing merit in mere survival. I used to think it was defiance but now I see it as lack of bloody ambition. We should have waged more wars. That's what you have to do to make people sit up and take notice. Wage a *fucking war!*"

The woman with the screaming toddler looked over from the next table and Cerwyn realised he had been ranting too loudly.

He turned to face Miriam again.

"I haven't seen you in ages and here I go, off on my high horse again!"

Miriam sipped her Americano carefully in case she singed her lips.

"Do you still see Leah?"

"Sometimes. Not often. It's for the best I suppose. I must have driven her mad over the years so I can't blame her. She's in Derby now. With her sister. I miss her sometimes. Not as much as I thought I would though. It was as if something had been cut loose from me and I suddenly felt lighter. I'm sure she felt the same. I still see Llew though. Your lad did the right thing though Miriam. Get away from this place as soon as you can. It drags you down with it. Where is he?"

"London. Works for some advertising firm. Don't ask me what he does. I can't understand it. Far too technical. He did try to explain it to me once but I told him not to bother. I'm far too old for all that technology. I find it hard enough to manage the remote control."

"But he comes home?"

"Not as often as I'd like but I don't complain. I know he's busy.

He takes me down to St Ives every year for a week. He knows I like Cornwall. We used to go there when he was little. He's booked somewhere different this year though. Says I need a change. Too set in my ways he says. Bless him. So we're going to Norfolk."

Miriam looked out of the window and, noticing that the rain had stopped, she reached for her shopping bag but Cerwyn leant forward, pushed away his coffee and placed his hand on hers.

"It was always you," he said. "All the time. Through it all. You know that don't you Miriam? It was always you."

She looked at him for a couple of seconds before gently moving his hand away. She picked up her bag, smiled at him and walked out, turning left in the direction of the new multi-storey car park.

FIFTY NINE

"You're too close!"

We'd been driving for something like twenty minutes in complete silence apart from the TomTom's occasional command to 'turn left' or to 'drive on designated route' so Miriam's sudden comment jolted me out of my semi-catatonic state.

"Look," she said, gripping the sides of her seat as if she was on a rocket. "You're virtually up that lorry's backside. This isn't London you know!"

I glanced at the TomTom screen. It said we had nine miles to our destination. We'd been stuck behind the lorry for ages and the road was winding. Trying to curb my impatience I eased down gently on the brake and allowed a gap of ten to fifteen yards to form between us.

"That's better," said Miriam, relaxing her grip on the seat.

The TomTom told me to take the next left. Miriam looked out of the window and sighed sulkily.

"Why are we coming this way anyway? I saw a motorway earlier. The same one we came along when we arrived."

"I just thought this might be more scenic."

"Well it isn't. It's very flat. Nothing much to see."

I flicked the indicator to take the left turn and was relieved to see that the lorry was going straight ahead. We suddenly found ourselves on a deserted country road with no markings.

"Are you sure this is the right way?"

The Norfolk trip hadn't been a great success. The weather had been grey, Miriam declared quite early on that she didn't like boats, she had refused point-blank to go on a trip along the Norfolk Broads so we had sat on a bench instead and watched the boats go by whilst eating ice cream and dodging wasps. In Miriam's opinion Great Yarmouth had been 'too common' and the yobs on the pier had kept her awake all night. The hotel manager had moved her to a room at the back but then she had moaned about there being no view. St Ives wasn't like this. That's what she kept saying. Next year we were going back to St Ives. She would go on her own if she had to. She knew what she liked and she didn't like Norfolk.

We drove along the bumpy road in silence again for half a mile or so before she spoke again.

"*He's* there you see."

"Who?"

"Your father. That's why I decided against the bungalow. He's there in Bryn Hyfryd with me."

She pulled down the sun-shade, checked her teeth for some reason and then pushed the sun-shade back up.

"I talk to him every day you know."

"I've heard you Mum. Don't worry. It's normal."

The TomTom told me it was recalculating.

"Does that mean we're lost?"

"We're fine."

"It certainly *looks* as if we're lost. There's grass in the middle of this road. It's like the ends of the earth! Turn round. Let's go home."

I wasn't entirely convinced that I knew where I was going either but I didn't want to show it. I decided that I would go down the bumpy road for another mile or so and, if it proved to be a dead end, I would admit my mistake and turn around. All the time the TomTom insisted that it was recalculating. When it told me to do a U-turn where safe to do so I switched it off.

"What have you done that for?"

"It was annoying me."

"You're annoyed by anything that tells you you're wrong. Just like your father."

There were seagulls. I opened the window a little and I could smell the sea in the air even though I couldn't see it.

.

SIXTY

We emerged from a small wood and found ourselves driving along a cliffside road. The sun came out and the North Sea was like a huge blue plate below us.

"Oh, isn't that lovely!" said Miriam.

"Told you Norfolk was beautiful."

She turned to me.

"So why didn't we come here instead of that horrible Yarmouth place? It's always the same isn't it? You only see the nice bits on your very last day. Just when you're on your way home."

"Want to stop for a bit?"

"No, it looks too blowy."

We drove along the road for a few hundred yards. A farmhouse appeared in the distance and I wondered if it was the one. I saw a woman coming out and waving at us. There was a dog circling excitedly around her feet. I slowed down. Then stopped.

"What are you doing?" said Miriam.

I unclicked my seat belt as the woman came up. The dog was barking by her side. The woman was about my age.

"Just undo your seat belt Mum."

I got out of the car and shook hands with the woman while the dog sniffed my leg.

"Sorry we're late," I said. "The TomTom went a bit mad outside Lowestoft."

"I'm amazed you found it at all," said the woman, watching as Miriam emerged suspiciously from the BMW. "You can imagine we don't get many visitors." She raised her voice a little and went over to Miriam. "Kelly," she said, extending her hand. "So pleased to meet you."

Miriam shook her hand and offered a polite but guarded smile. She glanced at me and there was more than a trace of discomfort in it.

"Pleased to meet you too," she said. "I'm Miriam."

"I know."

The dog barked and Miriam flinched, stepping back and almost falling into a hedge.

"He won't harm you," said Kelly. "*Snap! Be quiet boy!* He's just a bit boisterous." She bent down and stroked her dog gently. "He'll come to his senses in a minute. I'd offer you a cup of tea and some food but maybe that could wait because now is actually a perfect time if you'd like to come? This way. Snap will show us. Won't you boy? Go on!"

The path led along the clifftop. It was a mere strip of trodden down grass leading through taller tufts which swayed like dancing banshees in the wind.

"It's a real struggle getting the wheelchair up here," said Kelly over her shoulder, "but it's not too bad in the summer. We don't come in the winter of course. No matter how hard he protests!"

Snap was barking wildly up ahead.

"He's found him," said Kelly, smiling and increasing her pace. "I'll go and tell him you're here. He'll be so thrilled. I can't believe it!"

SIXTY ONE

The man in the wheelchair was wrapped up in a coat and scarf. Snap had flopped down beside him, his tongue hanging over the side of his mouth like a ribbon. The man was bald and looked very thin, almost skeletal. He was muttering to himself but none of the words were intelligible.

"He's had a good day today," said Kelly, raising her voice for his benefit. "Haven't you Daddy? You had a nice breakfast and then me and Snap took you up here. To your favourite spot. Now, are you warm enough?"

The man in the wheelchair looked up as she tightened the scarf a little and adjusted his coat but he didn't stop muttering to himself. His hands were shaking.

"I've brought some visitors to see you."

The man turned to us. I smiled and nodded.

"Nice to meet you," I said, politely and nervously. "Lovely day."

Miriam looked at me.

"He had a stroke about two years ago," said Kelly, wiping the long strands of red hair away from her face. "Since then he's been confined to this chair but he gets good days and bad. Sometimes he knows who I am and where he is. Sometimes he's in a fog. Nasty things strokes. They take away your body and steal your soul. He forgets so many things but he remembers the important stuff. I show him old photos of my mother once in a while and a little smile lights up on his face. I suppose one blessing of the stroke was that it took the edge off the grief."

"She passed away?" asked Miriam.

"Six years ago."

"I'm sorry to hear that."

Kelly nodded her appreciation. Then she turned to me.

"He was so thrilled to get your letter. I had to explain it to him of course but I could tell he was excited. I think he'd given up all hope."

"All hope of what?" asked Miriam.

Kelly looked at her.

"Of ever seeing you again."

SIXTY TWO

"I'm not sure if he ever thought you'd ever read it," said Kelly. "He told me about it many years later. He wasn't sure why he did it and said it was a silly mistake because you'd got married and had a baby and everything had changed. He was leaving Ireland and moving over to England, here to Norfolk, and there must have been part of him that wanted you to know where he was and what you meant to him. Even when you never replied he still loved you Miriam. I don't think a part of him ever truly stopped."

Forgetting everything about the damp grass and the stupid dog Miriam fell to her knees next to the wheelchair and took the man's hands in hers.

"Pádraig?"

He turned to her and smiled. He gripped her hand as tightly as he could. Then he motioned urgently to his daughter.

"What is it, Daddy?"

He muttered and grunted, nodding forcefully in the direction of the tall grass which waved all around them. He said something which I couldn't understand. But his daughter did.

"Grass? What on earth would you want some grass for?"

But he was determined. He stamped his feet and said the word again. Only louder this time.

"All right" said Kelly. "No need to make a scene!"

She ripped out a tuft of wild grass and gave it to Pádraig.

"Here you go."

He snatched the tuft of grass and immediately began to twist and pull at it, grunting at intervals, his tongue pushed tightly into the corner of his mouth.

"What on earth are you doing Daddy?"

He tied up the various strands of grass until it looked vaguely like a tiny man. He held it up. Offered it to Miriam. She took it as gratefully as if it was a beautiful bouquet of flowers.

"A straw bobby," she said.

Pádraig bounced in his chair again and produced strange guttural tones of excitement and pleasure. He urged Kelly for more grass.

"More?" she said. "How many of these things are you going to make?"

"Enough to fill a house," said Miriam, quietly. "A small cottage maybe. Although definitely not a mansion."

ACKNOWLEDGEMENTS

The author would like to thank Jacci Parry, Deborah Perkin, Catrin Beard, Shannon Cullen and Jon Gower for their help, guidance and support.

AUTHOR NOTE

Born in Bangor, Euron Griffith has a Creative Writing MA from the University of Glamorgan. Between 2011 and 2016 he published three novels in Welsh – *Dyn Pob Un*, *Leni Tiwdor* and *Tri Deg Tri*, and a children's novel *Eilian a'r Eryr*. His English language short story collection, *The Beatles in Tonypandy* appeared in 2017. Griffith lives in Cardiff, where he works as a radio and tv producer and plays in a band. This is his first novel in English.